# It's Harlequin's 60th anniversary this year!

**Harlequin Romance is going to shower you with…
diamond proposals and dazzling weddings,
sparkling brides and gorgeous grooms!**

DIAMOND BRIDES

*The Australian's Society Bride*
by Margaret Way

*Her Valentine Blind Date*
by Raye Morgan

*The Royal Marriage Arrangement*
by Rebecca Winters

*Two Little Miracles*
by Caroline Anderson

*Manhattan Boss, Diamond Proposal*
by Trish Wylie

*The Bridesmaid and the Billionaire*
by Shirley Jump

Whether it's the stunning solitaire ring that he's offering, the beautiful white dress she's wearing or the loving vows between them, these stories will bring a touch of sparkle to your life.

Dear Reader,

This is the year Harlequin celebrates its diamond anniversary! How amazing is that? And I think it's testimony to how many hearts have been touched across the world that an Irish gal like me gets to celebrate with them a half a world away from where the company began.

For me, one of the best things about Harlequin is that, in a busy world filled with so much to depress us, it's a company founded on love. I think that's just the most wonderful, wonderful thing. This is a company that says it's all right to dream, it's all right to fantasize, and it's more than all right to hope for and to believe in love. And it's a company that says, loudly, we love bringing you what you love to read. Those who write, those who edit, those who market, those who read—we all believe in love. So to be even a small part of that is the biggest thrill for me.

It's a sisterhood of sorts, I suppose, or a sorority. So welcome to the club, my friend. Long live love! And here's to another sixty years!

H's and K's,

*Trish*

# TRISH WYLIE

## *Manhattan Boss, Diamond Proposal*

DIAMOND BRIDES

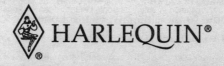

HARLEQUIN®

TORONTO • NEW YORK • LONDON
AMSTERDAM • PARIS • SYDNEY • HAMBURG
STOCKHOLM • ATHENS • TOKYO • MILAN • MADRID
PRAGUE • WARSAW • BUDAPEST • AUCKLAND

For Marilyn,
the kind of reader who makes me remember why
I write, even on the days words are hard to find…

And for John—
the best tour guide in New York City.

Recycling programs
for this product may
not exist in your area.

ISBN-13: 978-0-373-17569-7
ISBN-10: 0-373-17569-8

MANHATTAN BOSS, DIAMOND PROPOSAL

First North American Publication 2009.



This edition published by arrangement with Harlequin Books S.A.



www.eHarlequin.com

**Printed in U.S.A.**

**Trish Wylie** tried various careers before eventually fulfilling her dream of writing. Years spent working in the music industry, in promotions and teaching little kids about ponies gave her plenty of opportunity to study life and the people around her. Which, in Trish's opinion, is a pretty good study course for writing! Living in Ireland, Trish balances her time between writing and horses. If you get to spend your days doing things you love, then she thinks that's not doing too badly. You can contact Trish at www.trishwylie.com.

**Praise for Trish Wylie**

"Trish Wylie's *Her One and Only Valentine* has excellent characters—particularly the larger-than-life hero. It also has charm and wit to spare."
—*Romantic Times BOOKreviews*

Don't miss Trish Wylie's next Harlequin Romance
*His L.A. Cinderella*
July 2009

# PROLOGUE

'HE'S NOT COMING.'

'What do you mean he's not coming?'

Clare O'Connor turned away from the floor-length mirror, her chin lifting so she could search his eyes. Not that she knew him well enough to be able to read anything there. Tall, dark and brooding she'd named him after their first meeting. And despite the fact she'd since had glimpses of a wicked sense of humour, when he chose to use it, she still thought her initial impression was on the money.

She shook her head. 'What do you mean he's not coming? Did something happen to him?'

A muscle jumped in his jaw. And it was the first indication she had that he was telling the truth. She shook her head again, nervous laughter escaping her parted lips. No way. There was no way Jamie had done this to her. Not now.

'I'm sorry, Clare.'

When one long arm lifted towards her she stepped back, the world tilting a little beneath her feet. 'Where is he?'

'He's gone.'

'Gone?'

Gone where? Why? What had happened? This kind of thing didn't happen in real life! She tried to form a coherent thought rather than parroting everything she was told. Why now? Why not yesterday or the day before that or the day before that? When there'd been time to cancel everything and let everyone know. Why let her follow him all the way across the Atlantic if—?

'He didn't have the guts to face you.'

Clare laughed a little more manically. 'So he sent *you* to tell me?' Of all the people Jamie knew he had felt *this guy* was the one to send? It was almost funny. 'No phone call? No note? Is this a joke?'

'No joke. He's gone and he's not coming back.'

The determined tone to his voice made the edges of her vision go dark. When she felt herself swaying, two large hands grasped her elbows to steady her while she blinked furiously.

'You need to sit down.'

Clare yanked her arms free, her gaze focusing on a smudge of dirt on his jacket before sliding over the dark material and noticing several other smudges along the way. But she wasn't interested in how they'd got there, she just needed to think. She needed to—

When her chin jerked towards the door and her eyes widened with horror, his husky voice sounded above her head. 'I'll go.'

Dear God. All the people beyond that door, waiting for *her*—how was she supposed to face them? But she couldn't let him go out there and do her dirty work for her. Not that the offer wasn't tempting, but they were waiting for *her*. And some of them had flown thousands of miles—*for her.* So it was her responsibility to tell them…

Swallowing down a wave of nausea, she reached for his arm. 'Wait. Just give me a second here.'

Taking several deep breaths of cool air, she tightened her fingers around his forearm, as if the part of her that was drowning naturally sought out something solid to keep her from going under.

From somewhere she found the strength to keep her voice calm. 'Did he leave with her?'

'Clare—'

She flexed her fingers as she looked up. 'Did he? I want to know.'

'How long have you known?'

Up until he'd asked that question she'd never really known for sure. But she had her answer now, didn't she? So much for telling herself it was paranoia…

Letting go of his arm, she nodded firmly while biting down on her lower lip to stop it from trembling. If the price of naïveté was the death of the starry-eyed dreamer then the job was done. And she was about to receive her punishment on a grand scale, wasn't she?

'I'll tell them. It's because of me they're out there in the first place.'

'You don't have to.'

'Yes, I do.' An inward breath caught on a hint of a sob so she closed her eyes and willed it away, promising it: *later.* Later when no one could see. 'Jamie might not care about them but I do. They'll hear it from me.'

When she opened her eyes and glanced up, she saw what looked like respect in his eyes. And for some unfathomable reason she felt laughter bubbling up in her chest again—hysteria, probably. Possibly a hint of irony that it took something so completely degrading to earn respect from the man who had never approved of her in the first place.

When she lifted the front of her long skirt in both hands, he stepped back and opened the door for her, towering over her as she took a deep breath and hovered in the gap.

'I'm here if you need me.'

She smiled at him through shimmering eyes and then stepped forwards, her gaze focused on the flower-decked arch at the top of the room instead of the sea of faces turning her way.

It was the most humiliating day of her life.

'I'm afraid there won't be a wedding today…'

# CHAPTER ONE

'I'LL CALL YOU.'

*'Do.'*

Quinn opened his office door and looked up from the file he'd been reading, not entirely sure if it was the tail-end of the conversation or the sight of his personal assistant being hugged so tightly by some guy he'd never set eyes on before that brought a frown to his face. He should be aware of everything that happened in his own offices after all, shouldn't he? And he had the distinct niggling feeling he was being left out of the loop somehow—something he never, *ever* let happen.

Leaning his shoulder against the doorjamb, he watched with narrowed eyes until the stranger cut her loose.

'New boyfriend?'

The familiar lustrous sparkle of emerald eyes locked with his as the main door closed behind her mystery man. 'And when exactly do I have time for a boyfriend?'

'You know what they say about all work and no play.'

With a shake of her head, Clare bent to retrieve a

sheet of paper off her desk. So Quinn allowed his gaze to make a cursory slide over her tailored cream blouse and simple linen trousers, watching the subtle grace of her movement. If he'd been a romantic of any kind he'd have said Clare moved like a ballerina. She certainly had a ballerina's body: fine-boned and slender—a few more curves maybe, not that she ever dressed to flaunt them or that Quinn had ever looked closely enough to confirm their presence.

But since Quinn Cassidy had graduated with honours from the school of hard knocks he was somewhat lacking in anything remotely resembling romance. So if forced to use a word to describe the way she moved it would quite simply be feminine.

One of the things he'd liked right from the start was the fact she never felt the need to do anything to bring that femininity to a man's attention. It was also one of the many reasons she'd survived so long working as his PA. The one before her had barely had time to take off her jacket before she'd started leaning her cleavage towards him. It had been like sharing an office with a barracuda.

He shuddered inwardly at the memory.

'Speaking of work—' she calmly handed him a sheet of paper when he nudged off the doorjamb and took a step forwards '—here's a list of all the places you have to be today and when. Try and make a few of the appointments on time if you can—for a wee change.'

When she accompanied the words with a sideways tilt of her head and a small smirk that crinkled the bridge of her nose, Quinn couldn't help smiling, even though technically he was being told off. In fairness he didn't think his timekeeping had ever been bad, but in the year since Clare had come to work for him she'd been determined he should be at everything at least ten minutes early. He reckoned, however, that if he was early for every single meeting, and had to twiddle his thumbs while he waited for people to turn up, it would add up to a whole heap of wasted time in the long term.

So he rebelled regularly on principle.

He glanced over the neatly typed list before lifting his chin in time to watch Clare perch on the edge of her desk, a thoughtful expression on her face while she swung her feet back and forth. So he waited…

Eventually she spoke in the softly lilting Irish accent she hadn't lost since she'd come to New York. 'On the subject of *play*—it's been a while since I had to make a trip to Tiffany's…'

Quinn cocked a brow. 'And?'

She shrugged one shoulder. 'I just wanted to make sure I wasn't falling behind. Up till recently I'd been considering keeping a stock of those wee blue boxes here to save me some time.'

He watched as out of the corner of her eye she caught sight of an errant pen lying on the edge of the desk, giving it a brief frown before she dropped it into a nearby container with a satisfied smile. It never ceased to amaze him, the amount of pleasure she derived from the simplest of things.

'You're just missing your trips to Tiffany's.' He shook his head and looked her straight in the eye. 'I can't run all over Manhattan breaking hearts just so you can while away a few more hours down at your favourite store, now, can I?'

'Never stopped you before.' She thrust out her bottom lip and batted long lashes at him comically.

True. But he wasn't about to get drawn into another debate about his love life when he was suddenly much more interested in hers. 'So who was the Wall Street type?'

'Why?'

'Maybe I need to ask him what his intentions are towards my favourite employee…'

'So you get to vet all my boyfriends now, do you?'

Quinn folded his arms across his chest, allowing the corner of the sheet of paper to swing casually between his thumb and forefinger. 'You said he wasn't your boyfriend.'

Another shrug. 'He's not.'

She lifted her delicate chin and rose off the desk to walk round to her swivel chair, swinging forwards before informing him 'He's a client.'

Quinn knew what she was getting at, even if it apparently meant her part-time hobby had morphed into something bigger when he wasn't looking. 'This matchmaking game of yours is a business now, is it?'

'Maybe.' She drummed her neat fingernails on the sheaf of papers in front of her. 'Problem?'

Two could play at that game—she should know that by now—and her poker face wasn't worth squat, so Quinn continued looking her straight in the eye. 'Maybe.'

'Because it's during working hours or because you still think the whole thing is a great big joke? I'm not falling behind with my work, am I?'

The thought had never crossed his mind. Thanks to Clare, his working life ran like a well-oiled machine. Not that he hadn't managed to get things done before, but with her around everything was definitely less stressful than it had been before. There'd once been a time when he'd thrived on the adrenaline of being under pressure, but he'd outgrown those days. And, frankly, the matchmaking thing was starting to grate on him.

'I'd have thought you of all people would understand the danger of matching starry-eyed people with someone who might break their heart.'

It was a sucker punch, considering her history. But he knew Clare pretty well. If dozens of people came back to cry on her shoulder in a few months' time she'd feel responsible, and she'd silently tear herself up about it. She was digging her own grave. Quinn simply felt it was his responsibility to take the shovel out of her hand.

'C'mon, if they're so desperate they can't find a date without your help, then—'

Disbelief formed in her eyes. 'Is it so very difficult for you to believe that some people might simply be sick to death of trawling the usual singles scene? Not everyone has the—' she made speech marks with crooked fingers '—*success* you have with women…'

Quinn ignored the jibe. 'I s'pose that means I should expect to find long lines of Ugly Bettys and guys who still live with their mothers arriving in here every five minutes from here on in?'

If she thought for a single second he was going to be happy about that she could think again. He hadn't batted an eyelid when she'd matched up friends of mutual friends outside of work, but the line had to be drawn somewhere. And he was about to tell her as much when she pushed the chair back from her desk and walked to the filing cabinets.

'Don't worry, Quinn. If word keeps spreading as fast as it has these last few months, then pretty soon I'll be making enough money to be able to afford my own office. And then it won't be your problem any more, will it?'

'You're quitting on me now?'

The thought of the endurance test involved with breaking in another PA made him frown harder. Prior to Clare he'd gone through six in almost as many months.

'If you needed a raise all you had to do was say so…'

Clare continued searching the drawer. 'It's got nothing to do with getting a raise. It's a chance to build something on my own. And if I can help make a few people happy along the way, then all the better.'

Okay, so he could understand her feeling the need to stand on her own two feet. That part he got. But he'd been pretty sure the arrangement they had had been working for both of them. Why rock the boat?

Stepping over to the desk, he turned on his heel and sat down on the exact same spot Clare had, schooling his features and deliberately keeping his voice nonchalant.

'You've obviously been thinking about this for a while. So how come I'm only hearing about it now?'

'Maybe because you've never asked…'

'I'm asking now.'

It couldn't possibly be taking so long to find whatever it was she was looking for. Not with her hyperefficient filing system. Half the time he only had to think about information he needed and the next thing he knew, it was in front of him. She was avoiding looking at him, wasn't she?

'O'Connor—'

'You know, if you'd bothered reading the schedule I just gave you you'd see you have a meeting in less than twenty minutes…'

Nice try. Setting the schedule down, Quinn pushed upright and took the two strides necessary to bring him close enough to place his hands on her slight shoulders, firmly turning her to face him. When her long lashes lifted, her eyes searching each of his in turn, he did the same back before smiling lazily.

'Working for me proved too tough in the end, did it? If you recall, I warned you at the start I was no walk in the park.'

Clare's full mouth quirked at the edges—they both knew she dealt with him just fine, even on the days every other person on the planet would have avoided him.

'Well, I won't say there aren't days I have to bite my tongue pretty hard. But it's got nothing to do with the work—it's something I need to do for me. If I can make it here, I can make it anywhere.' Her smile grew. 'That's how the song goes, right?'

Quinn fought off another frown. 'So how much notice are you giving me?'

'Oh, I'm not handing in my notice just yet.'

But it was coming, wasn't it? She was serious. And her job had long since exceeded the usual remit of personal assistant. She was his girl Friday—co-ordinating the Clubs, making sure staffing levels were sufficient, putting together promotions, booking live acts, filling in when someone was sick even if it meant working for fifteen hours straight…

Everyone who worked for him had even taken to *calling* her 'Friday', and she always smiled when they did, so Quinn had assumed she was happy in the role she'd taken on. The thought that she *wasn't* happy irritated him no end. He should have known if she wasn't.

And how exactly was he supposed to list all she did for him in a Help Wanted ad if she *did* quit?

Realising his hands had slid downwards, his thumbs smoothing up and down on her upper arms while he thought, Quinn released her and stepped back. 'You'd miss all the craziness here, you know.'

Her voice softened. 'I will. I've loved it here.'

Despite the fact she'd just allayed one fear, it was the fact she hadn't used 'I would' or 'I might' but *'I will'*, that got to him most.

But he hid behind humour. 'I'd better think about making a trip to Tiffany's on my own to get one of those blue boxes for you, then, hadn't I?'

The smile lit up her face, making the room immediately brighter than it already was, with the summer sun filtering in between the Manhattan high-rises to stream through the large windows lining one wall.

'You should probably know I have a wish list…'

'And I'll just bet there's a diamond or two on it.'

She nodded firmly. 'Diamonds are a girl's best friend, they say. But don't go overboard.' She patted his upper arm. 'I haven't had to suffer my way through the usual broken heart required to get a blue box from you.'

Files in hand, she walked back to her desk, silently dismissing him even before she lifted an arm to check her wristwatch. 'Twelve minutes now—and counting.'

He stepped over to retrieve the schedule, and his gaze fell on the bright daisies she had in a vase on her desk. Like a trail of breadcrumbs, they were everywhere she spent any time—the simple flowers almost a reflection of her bright personality. Anywhere he saw daisies they reminded him of Clare.

When he didn't move she looked up at him with an amused smile. 'What now?'

'I can't stand in my own reception area for five minutes if I feel like it?'

'No—you can't. I have work to do. And my boss will give me hell if it isn't done.'

Another frown appeared on his face while he went into his office to retrieve the jacket he'd left lying over a chair, remaining in place until he stopped at the glass doors etched with his company's name.

'We're still going to Giovanni's later, right?'

Clare's head lifted and there was a brief moment of hesitation while she studied his face, confusion crossing her luminous eyes.

'Of course we are. Why?'

'Want me to come back for you?'

'*No-o.* I think I can manage to make it back to Brooklyn on my own—always have before.' She dropped her head towards one shoulder, still examining his face. 'Did you get out of some poor woman's bed on the wrong side this morning? You're being weird.'

'That's what I get for trying to be thoughtful? No wonder I don't do it that often…'

Clare lifted her arms and tapped the face of her watch with her forefinger, silently mouthing the words, *Ten minutes…*

'You see, now—*that* I won't miss when you're gone.'

She smiled a smile that lifted the frown off his face. 'I'm not leaving the country, Quinn. You'll still see me. And we'll always have Giovanni's on a Wednesday night—it's set in stone now.'

When he stayed in the open doorway for another thirty seconds she laughed softly, the shake of her head dislodging a strand of bright auburn hair from the loose knot tied at the nape of her neck. 'Would you go away? I have just as much to do as you do. And I'll have even more to do if I have to answer phone calls all day from people wondering why you're late—which you already are cos there's no way you're making it to that meeting in eight minutes.'

'Wanna bet?'

She rolled her eyes. 'Five bucks says you don't.'

'Aw, c'mon—it's hardly worth my while stepping through this door for five measly bucks.'

'If you don't step through that door it'll cost you that much in cab fare to the nearest hospital.'

He fought off a chuckle of laughter at the empty threat. 'Loser picks up the tab for dinner.'

'You're on. Now, go away. Shoo.' She waved the back of her hand at him.

Reaching for his cellphone as he headed for the elevators, Quinn realized he'd miss their daily wagers. He liked things the way they were. Why did he have to have his life knocked off balance again? Hadn't he spent half of it on an uneven enough keel already? And it wasn't that he didn't understand her need to build something, but the dumb matchmaking thing wasn't the way to go. Not for Clare. Not in his opinion.

'Mitch—Quinn Cassidy—I'm on a tight schedule today, can you meet me halfway?'

See—sometimes in order to win a bet a guy had to bend the rules a little—play dirty if necessary. Occasionally he even had to get creative. And Quinn liked to think he was a fairly creative kind of guy when the need arose. Plenty of women had benefited from that creativity and none of them had ever complained…

He'd find a way to make Clare see sense about the matchmaking—he just needed the right opening, and it was for her own good after all. She'd thank him in the long run.

*What were friends for?*

## CHAPTER TWO

'YOU KNOW, I THINK I'LL have dessert.' Quinn patted his washboard-flat stomach as he came back to the table, smiling wickedly in Clare's direction.

'You *cheated.*'

'You said I'd be late—I wasn't—*I won.*'

Clare couldn't hold back the laughter that had been brewing inside her all evening, thanks to his ridiculous level of gloating. But then he'd always been able to draw laughter out of her, even when he was being so completely shameless.

'I need someone else to hang out with twelve hours a day.' She glanced around to see if any of their friends, seated round the table, would take up her offer. 'Anyone?'

'Nah, I'm irreplaceable.' Turning his chair with one large hand, he sat down, forearms resting on the carved wooden back while he dangled the neck of his beer bottle between long fingers with his palm facing upwards.

'She tell you she quit her job today?' The bottle swayed back and forth while startlingly blue eyes examined each of their faces in turn; a smile flirting with the corners of his mouth.

'Don't listen to him.'

Erin smiled. 'Oh, honey, we never do.'

There was group laughter before Quinn continued in the rumbling, husky-edged voice that made most women smile dumbly at him. 'Yup, she's dumping me to go help the sad and the lonely.'

'Leaving *you* sad and lonely?'

Clare laughed softly when Evan took her side with his usual deadpan expression. 'He'd never admit it out loud but he'd miss me, you know…'

'Rob and Casey got engaged.' Madison smiled an impishly dimpled smile when Clare's face lit up. 'That's three now, isn't it?'

'Four.' Clare almost sighed with the deep sense of satisfaction it gave her. 'And I've had ten referrals in as many days.'

'You're charging the new fee you talked about?'

She nodded. 'And I talked to a website designer yesterday. He reckons we can have a site put together in a month or so—soon as I'm ready.'

'Make sure there's a disclaimer somewhere.' Quinn rumbled in a flat tone.

Clare scowled at him. 'Just because you don't believe in love in the twenty-first century doesn't mean other people don't.'

His dark brows quirked just the once, his gaze absent-mindedly sweeping the room. 'Never said I don't believe in it.'

Clare snorted in disbelief. 'Since when?'

Attention slid back to her and he held her questioning gaze with a silent intensity that sent an unfamiliar shiver up her spine.

'So if I'm not married by thirty-four it automatically means I don't believe in it, does it?'

'You only believe in it for *other people...*'

And, come on, he couldn't even say the word out loud, could he? Not that she doubted he felt it for family and friends, but when it came to Quinn and *women...* well...they probably cited him in the dictionary under 'love 'em and leave 'em'.

Without breaking his gaze, he lifted a hand to signal a waitress—as if he had some kind of inner radar that told him where she was without him having to look. Or more likely because he knew waitresses in restaurants had a habit of watching him wherever he went. They were women after all,

'I could throw that one right back at you.'

It was just as well he was sitting out of smacking distance, because he knew why she wasn't as starry-eyed about love as she'd once been. Not that she didn't believe she might love again one day. She'd just be more sensible about it next time. It was why the method she used for matchmaking made such sense to her. Didn't mean his words didn't sting, though...

And now he was putting her back up. 'If you believe in it, then how come you have such a problem with me doing what I do?'

Quinn broke the visual deadlock to order dessert with a smile that made the young waitress blush, and then attempted to drum up support. 'C'mon, guys—tell her I'm right. People will blame her when they don't end up riding off into the sunset on a white horse.'

Clare dipped her head towards one shoulder, a strand of hair whispering against her cheek while she blinked innocently. 'Aren't you always right? I thought that was the general impression you liked people to have.'

There was chuckling around the table, but Quinn's

expression remained calm, inky-black lashes brushing lazily against his tanned skin. 'I'm right about *this.*'

'You're a cynic.'

'I'm a *realist.*'

'You don't have a romantic bone in your body.'

A dangerously sexy smile made its way onto his mouth, light dancing in his eyes. 'I have a few dozen women you can call who'd disagree with that.'

Clare rolled her eyes while the male contingent at the table laughed louder and the women groaned. 'Whatever miracle it is you pull with women it has nothing to do with romance—it's got more to do with your *availability.*'

'I keep telling you I'm available, but do you take advantage of me? Oh no...'

It was impossible not to react. And since it was either gape or laugh, she went with the latter. Quinn could say the most outrageous things, smile that wicked smile of his, and he *always* got away with it. He was that guy a girl's mother warned her about: the devil in disguise.

Clare could hardly be blamed for having had the odd moment of weakness when she'd wondered what it would be like to flirt a little with someone like him. Thankfully, with age came the wisdom of experience. And she'd been burned by a devil in disguise once already, hadn't she?

She smiled sweetly. 'You see, I *would*, but I hate queues.'

'I'd let you jump the line, seeing we're friends...'

'Gee, thanks.'

'You believe in love at first sight now as well, I s'pose?' Erin leaned her elbows on the chequered tablecloth and challenged Quinn.

'Nope.' He shook his head and lifted his hand to draw a mouthful of liquid from the moisture-beaded bottle. 'Lust at first sight? That's a different story.'

He clinked his bottle with Evan's in a display of male bonding that made Clare roll her eyes again.

'And we wonder why you three are still single.'

Quinn's face remained impassive. 'I still maintain you can't use the 'finding soulmates' tag line on business cards. It's false advertising…'

'Soulmates *exist*—you ask anyone.' She reached for her wine glass while Erin and Rachel agreed with her.

Quinn nodded. 'Yep, right up there with chubby cherubs carrying bows and arrows. They had a real problem with one of them stopping traffic on East Thirtieth a while back—it was on CNN…'

Morgan almost choked on a mouthful of beer.

Taking a sip of wine and swirling the remaining liquid in her glass while she formulated a reply, Clare waited until Quinn had thanked the waitress for his slice of pie.

And then, despite deeply resenting the fact that she felt the need to justify her fledgling business, she kept her tone purposefully determined. 'Soulmates are simply people who are the right fit for each other. That means finding someone with common goals and needs, someone who wants what you want out of life and is prepared to stick with you for the long haul, even when things get tough—'

'You go, girl!'

Madison winked while Clare kept her gaze fixed on Quinn, watching him stare back with a blank expression so she couldn't tell what he thought of her mission statement.

She persisted. 'What I do is put a person looking for commitment with someone who feels the same way they do about life. That's all. Whether or not it works is up to them. I'm the middle man in a business deal, if you want to put it in terms you'll understand.'

Quinn's eyes narrowed a barely perceptible amount. 'And now who's the cynic?'

She set her glass down on the table and leaned forwards. 'If I was a cynic would I even bother in the first place? People need other people, Quinn; it's a fact of life.'

'And meeting the right guy's not easy—you ask any girl in New York.'

Erin's words raised a small smile from Clare. 'No, it's not. But men in the city find it just as tough as the women, especially when they *both* have busy careers.'

Quinn set his bottle lightly on the table, lifting a fork. 'You don't feel the need to go out and date any, though, do you? Hardly a good ad for your business: the matchmaker who can't find a match…I think this is your way of avoiding getting back in the game when everybody at this table thinks it's about time you did.'

Clare gritted her teeth. He could be *so* annoying when he put his mind to it.

'Clare will date when she's ready to—won't you, hon?' Madison smiled a smile that managed to translate as sympathy into Clare's eyes.

But Clare didn't need any help when it came to dealing with Quinn. She'd been doing it long enough not to be fazed. 'It's not that I'm not ready, it's—'

'Jamie wasn't a good example of American guys, O'Connor—you need to get back out there.'

The words drew her gaze swiftly back to his face, and her answer was laced with rising anger. 'And how am I supposed to find the time to date anyone when I spend so much time with *you*?'

It stunned the table into an uneasy silence; all eyes focused on Quinn as he frowned in response. 'So I'm your cover now, am I?'

She opened her mouth, but he'd already shrugged and returned his attention to his plate, digging forcefully with the edge of his fork. 'Funny how it hasn't stopped *me* finding time to date in the last year.'

Now, *there* was the understatement of the century! Without looking round the table to confirm it, Clare felt five pairs of eyes focusing on her. Waiting…

She damped her lips before answering. 'So long as the relationship doesn't last more than five or six weeks, right?'

The eyes focused on Quinn, who shrugged again. 'You know by then if there's any point wasting your time or theirs.'

'And you're too busy to waste any time, right?' Which kind of proved her point.

'Still made the time to begin with, didn't I?'

Okay, he had her on that one. But before she could get herself out of the hole she'd apparently just dug for herself, he added, 'Maybe I should just save myself some of that precious time by getting you to find my 'soulmate' for me. Then I can settle down to producing another generation of heartbreakers and you can stop using me as a stand-in husband.'

Clare inhaled sharply, her lips moving to form the name for him that had immediately jumped into the front of her brain.

But Erin was already jumping to her defence. 'That was uncalled-for, Quinn.'

'Yet apparently overdue.' The fork clattered onto the side of his plate before he leaned back, lifting his arms and arching his back in a lazy stretch. 'Can't fix a problem if I don't know it exists in the first place, can I?'

He said it calmly, but Clare knew he wasn't happy. So she made an attempt at humour to defuse the situation before it got out of hand. 'And why bother finding a wife when I fill eight out of ten criteria for the job every day, right?' She added a small smile so he'd know she was kidding. 'Maybe I'm *your* cover?'

The corners of his mouth twitched. 'Okay, then, since we're in such an unhealthy relationship—you find my mythical soulmate and I'll not only get out of your way, I'll get off your case about the matchmaking too.'

Evan's deep voice broke the sudden stunned silence with words that would seal her fate: 'She'll never in a million years find someone for *you* to settle down with.'

*And that did it*—Clare had had enough of her fledgling business being the butt of the guys' jokes. So it was a knee-jerk reaction.

'Wanna bet?' She folded her arms across her breasts and lifted a brow at Evan. But when Evan held his hands up in surrender, she looked back at Quinn. To find him smiling the merest hint of a smile back at her, as if he'd just won some kind of victory.

So she lifted her chin higher, to let him know he hadn't won a darn thing. 'Well?'

'You win, you can do matchmaker nights at the clubs and I'll split the door with you.'

*What?* Her heart raced at the very idea, a world of

possibilities growing so fast in her mind that she skimmed over the fact that the offer had been made so quickly. Almost as if he'd planned what to wager before the bet had been made. But she wasn't blinded enough by the business potential not to ask the obvious. 'And if I lose?'

Quinn cocked his head. 'Having doubts about your capabilities already, O'Connor?'

'Simply making the terms clear in front of witnesses. And if you're trying to claim you've only been playing the field all these years because you haven't met the right girl, then I guarantee you—I'll find you a girl who can last way longer than six weeks…'

'Wanna bet?' The smile grew.

Which only egged her on even more. 'I think we've already established that.'

Though she couldn't help silently admitting her unknown forfeit was scaring her a little. She'd call the whole thing off if her payoff wasn't so huge, and if he just didn't have that look in his eyes that said he had her right where he wanted her…

'I'm starting a pool—who's in?' There were several mumbled answers to Morgan's question.

None of which Clare caught because she was too busy silently squaring off with Quinn, neither of them breaking the locked gazes that signalled a familiar battle of wills. Well, she was no push-over these days, so if he thought she was backing down now they'd gone this far in front of an audience he was sorely mistaken.

'If you lose…'

She held her breath.

'It's a blind forfeit.'

Meaning he could chose anything he wanted when

it was done? *Anything?* He had to be kidding! She could end up cleaning his house for months, or wearing clown shoes to work, or—well, the list was endless, wasn't it?

He continued looking at her with hooded eyes, thick lashes blinking lazily and silent confidence oozing from every pore of his rangy body. And then he smiled.

Damping her dry lips, she looked round at the familiar faces, searching each one for a hint of any sign they'd see what was happening as a joke and let it slide so she could get out of trouble.

*No such luck.*

'You could just admit I'm right about this business idea of yours and let it go. Keep it as a hobby if you must. That'd give you more time for dating, right?'

With a deep breath she stepped over the edge of what felt distinctly like a precipice. 'No limit on the number of dates. And once you hit the six weeks without a Tiffany's box I automatically win.'

'Fine, but if I say it's not working with one we move on. I'll give you...' his gaze rose to a point on the ceiling, locking with hers again when he had an answer '...three months to find Little Miss Perfect.'

'Six.'

'Four.'

'Five.'

'Four from the first date...'

It was the best she was going to get and she knew it. *'Done.'*

There was a flurry of activity as their friends sought out a pen, and Morgan used the back of a napkin to place their bets. And in the meantime Quinn had Clare's undivided attention while he slowly made his way round to her, hunkering down and examining her eyes before extending one large hand, his husky-edged voice low and disturbingly intimate.

'Shake on it, then.'

Clare turned in her seat and looked at his outstretched hand, her pulse fluttering. She damped her lips again, and took another deep breath, before lifting her palm and setting it into his. Her voice was equally low when she looked up into his eyes.

'Cheat this time and you're a dead man.'

A larger smile slid skilfully into place a split second before his incredible eyes darkened a shade, and long fingers curled until her smaller hand was engulfed in the heat of his. But instead of shaking it up and down to seal the deal he simply held on, rubbing his thumb almost unconsciously across the ridges of her knuckles. Then his voice dropped enough to merit her leaning closer to hear him, and the combined scent of clean laundry and pure Quinn overwhelmed her,

'Don't have to. Cos either way I win—*don't I*?'

# CHAPTER THREE

QUINN SINCERELY DOUBTED he'd be asked as many questions if he applied to join the CIA. Who knew proving his point was going to involve so much darn paperwork? It was a deep and abiding hatred of paperwork that had merited a PA in the first place…

Swinging his office chair back and forth while he read through the rest of Clare's questionnaire, he wondered why she couldn't just have answered the majority of them herself. Because if working together and spending time together socially wasn't enough, then the fact she'd lived in the basement apartment of his Brooklyn Heights brownstone for the last eleven months should have given her more than enough information.

She knew him as well as anyone he hadn't grown up with ever had; it was a proximity thing.

Lifting the folder off his desk, he challenged gravity by leaning further back in his chair, twirling his pen in and out of his fingers and laughing out loud when he discovered: *How important is sex in a relationship?*

It even came with a rating system. Unfortunately he didn't think the rating went high enough for most men.

'It's not supposed to be funny.'

Rocking the chair forwards, he swung round to face the door where Clare was standing with her arms folded. In fairness he thought she'd done well to stay away for as long as she had. He'd had the questionnaire for a whole ten minutes already.

'Aw, c'mon, O'Connor. Not only is it funny, you gotta admit some of it's pretty darn pointless too.'

'Like what, exactly?'

With a challenging cock of his head he wet his thumb and forefinger and loudly flicked back two pages, looking down to quote. '"Do you feel it's important that the man earns more money than the woman"?'

When he looked up Clare was scowling. 'Some people think that's important—you'd be surprised how many men feel emasculated if the woman earns more than they do.'

He nodded sagely. 'You know the *pathetic* rating on all your male clients just went up a couple dozen notches right there, don't you?'

'Spoken by the man who sends a gift from Tiffany's as a goodbye. Money is hardly an issue for you, is it?'

'I never felt like less of a man when I didn't have any. Money's not what makes a man a man. Women who think that aren't interested in who he really is.' He looked down and flicked over another page. 'And another one of my personal favourites: "Do you feel pets can act as a substitute family?"' Lifting his chin, he added, 'Shouldn't you ask about dressing them up in dumb outfits and carrying them around in matching bags?'

'Not everyone wants children.'

'Why don't you just *ask that*, then?'

Swiftly unfolding her arms, she marched across the room and reached for the edge of the questionnaire. 'It's on page five. I knew you weren't taking this seriously. You've no notion of finding the right girl.'

Quinn held the questionnaire out of her reach behind his head, fighting off the need to chuckle. 'I'm taking this very seriously. You just might want to think about tailoring the questions differently for men and women—no self-respecting guy is gonna read this without tossing it in the nearest wastepaper basket.'

Clare stood to her full five-seven, the look of consternation written all over her face making him feel the need to laugh again. But somehow he doubted she'd appreciate it, so he cleared his throat.

'I'm just giving you my professional opinion. You do questionnaires for the clubs' clientele all the time and none of them are ever this bad.'

'They have to be the same questions so I can put like-minded people together.'

'What happened to opposites attracting?'

'The things that matter have to match.' She folded her arms again. 'You can back out of this any time you want you know—just say the word and we can go back to the way we were before.'

Nice try. But it was attempting to get back to the way they were that had given him the dumb idea in the first place. It was the very opening he'd been looking for. There was no way he was letting her out of this one. And she was no more likely to find him a soulmate through a questionnaire than he was to start dressing pets in clothes. Not that he had time for pets right this minute but there was a dog somewhere in his future—a large dog—one docile enough to make a loyal friend for kids to climb all over.

He lowered his arm and flicked through the pages to see if he could find a question that asked about pets *and* kids. Every kid should have a dog, he felt—and, not having had one when he was a kid, Quinn had no intention of his own kids missing out. And, yes, he *would* be ticking the kids question on page five—he came from a large family—there had just better be a box that said 'some day'.

'If you're going to treat this like a big joke it'll never work. You have to give it a chance.'

'I already told you I'm taking it seriously.'

When she didn't say anything he looked up, momentarily caught off-guard by the cloud in her usually bright eyes. 'What?'

Clare pursed her lips and let them go with a hint of a *pop*, shifting her weight before her brows lowered and she finally asked, 'You're *genuinely* interested in meeting someone you can make an *actual* commitment to?'

What was that supposed to mean? He had a suspicion he wasn't going to like the way she was thinking. 'You don't think I'm capable of making an *actual* commitment?'

'I didn't say that.'

It was what she'd meant, though. And he'd been right. He didn't like what she thought one little bit. 'I'm financially secure, own my own home—in one of the highest-priced real estate areas outside of Manhattan, I might add—and I've already done more than my share of playing the field. Why wouldn't I want to make a commitment at some point?'

And now she was frowning in confusion, as if none of that had ever occurred to her before.

Quinn happened to think he was an all-round pretty great guy if you discounted his earlier years. The vast majority of women seemed to agree. And surely the very fact he'd resisted the kind of trouble that could have led him into a rapid downward spiral in his teens was testimony to his determination to make a better life for himself—and anyone who might end up sharing it.

Okay, so he wasn't a saint. Who was? But what had he done to rate so low in Clare's opinion?

Clenching his jaw, he turned his chair back to the long desk lining one wall, tossing the questionnaire down. 'I'll throw this your way before I go. And then we'll see if there's anyone out there prepared to take on this bad boy.'

'Quinn—'

'Send in the monthly accounts and get Pauley on the line for me.'

In all the time she'd worked for him he'd never once dismissed her the way he just had. But he'd be damned if he'd feel guilty about it after *that.*

The accounts were set gently in front of him.

'Thanks.'

'Pauley's on line two.'

He lifted the receiver, his hand hovering over the flashing light when she spoke, her lilting accent soft with sincerity. 'It's not that I think you *can't* make a commitment, Quinn. I just didn't realize you felt you were ready to. I'm sorry.'

Taking a deep breath of air-conditioned air, he set the receiver down and turned in his chair to look up at her. And the gentle smile he found there had him smiling back in a single heartbeat. But then she'd been able to do that ever since he'd got to know her better.

Sanding off the edges of a rough mood with her natural softness…

He could really have done with her being around for the decade of his life when he'd been angry every hour of every day, if she had that effect on him every time.

'We've never talked about any of this, that's all. And we're still pretty new to this friends thing, if you think about it.'

Clare nodded, her chin dropping so she could study the fingers she had laced together in front of her body before she looked at him from beneath long lashes. 'It's not felt that way in a long time.'

'I know.'

There was an awkwardness lying between them that hadn't been there in a long time either. Quinn felt the loss of their usual ease with each other, but he couldn't see how to fix it without continuing on the path he'd already taken.

'What happens after the questionnaire?'

Lowering his gaze, he caught sight of her mouth twitching before she lifted her chin. 'We have a sit down interview.'

His eyes narrowed. 'About what?'

'Dating etiquette…'

His eyes widened. She had to be yanking his chain. 'You think I don't know how to behave on a date?'

'It's *how* you behave we need to discuss.' And now she was fighting off laughter, wasn't she? He could see it in her eyes. 'Men and women can have very different expectations of dating.'

Quinn was at a loss for words. Now he wasn't just commitment-phobic, he didn't know how to treat a woman either? She probably thought he kicked kittens too.

'A lot of men expect a first date to end with—'

He held up a palm. 'That debate can wait.'

When her mouth opened, he pointed a long finger towards the door. 'Work now—deep water later. I don't pay Pauley to hang on the phone all day.'

Waiting until the door clicked shut behind her, he stared at the wood, and then ran a palm down over his face. If she thought he was discussing his sex life with her in that little sit-down interview of hers then she could think again. And if she was going to delve into his private life on any level beyond the one he'd given her access to, then she'd better be prepared for the turn-about is fair play rule. In fact she could go first. His mom had raised all the Cassidy boys to be mannerly—no matter how much they'd protested.

Actually, now he had time to think about it, getting to know her better appealed to him. There were plenty of things he'd like to know that he'd never asked because it felt as if he'd be crossing some kind of invisible chalk line. If he delved beneath the surface a little he could find out if she was hiding behind the matchmaking. And if she was?

Well. He could use that.

Not to mention the point he now had to make regarding his eligibility as potential long-term partner material, should he ever decide to settle down—which, in fairness, wasn't going to be any time soon.

But it was a matter of pride now…

All right, so she'd never believed her questionnaires were all that amusing until she started reading Quinn's that evening at home. It turned out knowing someone beforehand shed a whole new light on the answers—

some of them so blatantly Quinn they made her laugh out loud.

But then there were the other ones…

Ones that made her wonder if she knew him anywhere near as well as she'd thought she did, or if she'd ever made as much of an effort *trying* to get to know him as she should have. Thanks to the questionnaire, she wanted to know everything. Everything she might have missed or misconstrued. Even if she discovered along the way that the friend she had was an illusion she'd conjured up in her head. Like an invisible friend a small child needed after they'd gone through an emotional trauma they couldn't deal with alone.

On paper Quinn was quite the package: stupidly rich, scarily successful at everything he did, liked pets, wanted kids one day, supportive of a woman's need for a career as well as a family. Add all that to how he looked and it was a wonder he'd managed to stay single as long as he had…

It certainly wasn't for the lack of women trying to hunt him down.

Ever since she'd first been introduced to Quinn he'd been either in the company of or photographed with stunningly beautiful women. None of them she now knew, as his PA, lasted beyond the maximum six-week cut-off point before he backed off and Clare was told to send a little blue box. And miraculously, barring the few weeping females she'd had to lend a sympathetic ear to, Clare was unaware of any of them stalking him. But surely one of them would have been worth hanging on to?

Thing was, if he genuinely was ready to make a commitment to someone then she was going to have to take their bet more seriously.

When the phone beside her sofa rang she picked it up without checking the caller ID. 'Hello?'

'What you doing?'

For some completely unfathomable reason her pulse skipped at the sound of his familiar rough-edged voice. 'Talking to you on the phone. Why?'

It wasn't as if she could confess to committing all his questionnaire answers to memory, was it?

'Thought I'd come down for my interview.'

*Now?* Clare dropped her chin, her eyes widening at the sight of the minute cotton shorts and cropped vest she'd thrown on after her shower, *sans* underwear. Not that she'd ever felt the need to dress up to see him, but what she was wearing wasn't designed for *anyone's* eyes—not even her own in a mirror. It was a 'not going anywhere on a hot, humid summer's night' outfit.

'Are you home?' The slightly breathless edge to her voice made her groan inwardly.

'Yup, I'll bring down a bottle of something.'

'Erm…I'm not exactly dressed for company… You need to give me a minute.'

There was a pause.

Then, 'And now you know I need to know, right?'

The way his voice had lowered an octave did something weird to her stomach. And her lack of a reply gave him reason enough to ask the obvious: 'You *are* dressed right?'

'Stop that.'

'Well, at least I didn't use the tell me what you're wearing line.'

'You may as well have.' Feeling confident he wouldn't appear while he was upstairs on the phone, she curled her legs underneath her and settled back, wriggling deeper into the massive cushions as she smiled at the all-too-familiar banter. '*Friends* don't do that kind of phone call.'

After a heartbeat of a pause he came back with another rumbling reply, adding an intimacy to the conversation that unsettled her all over again. 'I'd consider it, with that lilting accent of yours. We could do one as part of the date training I'm apparently in need of.'

She shook her head against the edge of the sofa and sighed. 'I give up.'

''Bout time too. So tell me what you're wearing that's such a big problem.'

When a burst of throaty laughter made its way out of her mouth she clamped a hand over it to make sure nothing else escaped.

'C'mon…it can't be that bad. It's sweats two sizes too big, isn't it?'

She frowned, blinking at a random point on the wall over her mantel. Because, actually, she didn't think she wanted one of the most eligible bachelors in New York thinking she couldn't wear something sexy if she felt like it. Not that she was looking for a blue box of her own at any stage.

Widening her fingers enough to speak, she felt an inner mischievous imp take over. 'How do you know I'm not wearing something sexy I don't want you to see?'

When there was silence on the other end of the line she contemplated jumping off the Brooklyn Bridge out of embarrassment. And then, above the sound of her heart thundering in her ears, she heard an answer so low it was practically in the territory of pillow talk. 'Are you flirting with me? Cos if you *are*…'

If she was—*what*? She swallowed hard and summoned up the control to keep her voice calm as she risked removing her hand from her mouth. 'You're the one who said he wanted it to be a training call.'

Another long pause. 'A training call before a training date is a bit of a leap, don't you think?'

'I didn't start this.'

Terrific. Now she was an eight-year-old.

'I'd argue that, but let's just give this another try. What exactly is it you're wearing that means I can't come down there right this second?'

'You don't think I even *own* anything sexy, do you? When you think of me down here you automatically assume I'm dressed like a slob.'

'Can't say I've ever wondered what you were wearing down there before this phone call.'

The Brooklyn Bridge was getting more tempting by the second.

Then he made her stomach do the weird thing again by adding 'Always gonna wonder after this though. And any inappropriate thoughts I have will be entirely *your* fault. You're the girl next door—I'm never s'posed to think of you as anything but cute.'

'I'm the girl *downstairs*. And for your information I'm wearing something entirely too sexy to be considered cute.' She almost added a *so there*.

'Liar.' She could hear him smiling down the line. 'And don't pout. With those braids in it makes you look about sixteen.'

Clare shot upright and looked out of the French windows leading to their small garden. To find Quinn sitting on the stone steps, long legs spread wide and a bottle of wine tucked under one arm while two glasses dangled from his fingers as he grinned at her. She didn't even need to be closer to see the sparks of devilment dancing in the blue of his eyes. *The rat.*

He jerked his head. 'C'mon out. It's cooler now.'

'I don't drink wine with peeping Toms.' She smirked.

'I'm in my own backyard looking into an apartment *I own* and if you'd been naked I like to think you'd have had the sense to pull the drapes.'

She dropped her chin and looked down again.

There was another rumbling chuckle of laughter. 'I promise not to make a pass at you. We haven't even been on a training date yet.'

'That's not how it works.'

'No?'

Clare scowled at him. '*No.* It's a *discussion* about dating—not a dress rehearsal.'

'If you plan on winning this bet you might have to treat me as a special case.' He even had the gall to waggle his dark brows at her before jerking his head again. 'Come on.'

'I'm staying where I am—it's your dime.'

Quinn shrugged. 'Okay, then.'

Clare sighed heavily while he lodged the receiver between his ear and his shoulder. Tugging the loosened cork free from the bottle, he set the glasses down before lifting them one by one to pour the deep red liquid. Then he set the bottle at the bottom of the steps before leaning forwards to place a glass by the door.

Lifting the other glass, he pointed a long finger. 'That one's yours.'

'Can't reach it from here…'

'You'll have to come get it, then, won't you?'

'I'm good, thanks.'

'I'm not actually so desperate—'

*'Thanks for that.'* And, ridiculously, it hurt that he'd said it. 'A little tip for you, Romeo: don't use that line on any of the dates I send you on.'

'I was going to say, not so desperate I have to force myself on a woman. You really think I'm slime, don't you? When did that happen?'

Heat rising on her cheeks, she mumbled back, 'I don't think you're slime.'

'Good. Cos I was starting to wonder…'

Unable to hold his gaze for long, even from a distance, Clare frowned at the music she had playing in the background. It had been fine listening to the sultry tones when she'd been on her own, reading his questionnaire, but she really didn't need a romantic ambience now he was there in person—especially when she was feeling so irrational with him close by. So she lifted the control, aiming it at the CD player.

'No—leave it. I gave you that album for Christmas. Hardly likely to give you something I wouldn't like listening to, was I?'

Clare had discovered a lot of the music she loved thanks to Quinn's massive collection upstairs. When she'd first moved in she would hear it drifting downwards on the night air, and for weeks every morning conversation had started with 'What were you playing last night?'

Sometimes she'd even wondered if, after a while, he'd chosen something different every night just to keep her listening. It had become a bit of a Cassidy-O'Connor game.

'So, how'd I score on my questionnaire?'

The hand holding the controls dropped heavily to her

side. He really didn't miss a thing, did he? And there was no point trying to deny she'd been reading it when she still had it on her lap.

'It's not a *test.* Did you tell the truth all the way through it?'

'The whole truth and nothing but; didn't take the Fifth on a single one. Why?'

Clare shrugged, risking another look at him. 'There was some stuff I didn't know, that's all.'

The familiar lazy smile crept across his mouth, and his voice dropped again. 'Ahh, I see. Surprised you, did I?'

'Maybe a little…' She felt the beginnings of an answering smile twitching the edges of her mouth.

'I did say we were still pretty new to this friendship thing.'

'Yes, you did, but I really thought I knew you better. Now I feel like I wasn't paying enough attention.' When the confession slipped free of its own accord, her heart twisted a little in her chest, and her voice was lower as she followed the old adage of 'in for a penny'. 'And I'm sorry about that, Quinn—I really am. I should have been a better friend. You helped me out when I needed help most, when I was broke and jobless and about to become homeless. If you hadn't been there…'

Quinn's reply was equally low, and so gentle it made her heart ache. 'Don't do that.'

'But—'

'But nothing.' She heard him take a breath. 'I needed a PA; you needed a job. I had an empty apartment; you needed a place to live. It was good timing. And you were right to stay when you did. Don't second-guess that—it took guts to stay.'

Great, now she had a lump in her throat. She even had to look away long enough to blink her vision back into focus. What was with her tonight? She hadn't felt so vulnerable in a long, long while.

'Do you miss home, O'Connor?'

'I *am* home.' Clare frowned down at her knees when she realized how the statement could be misconstrued. After all, she couldn't keep living in Quinn's basement for ever any more than she could keep relying on the job he'd given her. It was well past the point where she should have been able to step out from underneath his protective wing.

'New York is home now.' She made an attempt at lightening the mood. 'And when I have lots of successful matchmaking nights at your clubs and half the door I can afford an apartment of my own, can't I?'

The teasing smile she shot his way was met with one of his patented unreadable expressions. 'Can't get away from me fast enough, can you?'

'I'm not trying to get away from you.'

'Looks that way…' He twisted the stem of the wine glass between his thumb and forefinger, dropping his gaze to study the contents. 'You need to be careful there, O'Connor. You might hurt my feelings…'

He threw her a grin, but Clare's heart twisted at the very thought of hurting him even the littlest bit. Not that she thought she ever could. It took a lot to get through Quinn's outer shell—ninety-nine point nine percent of things were water off a duck's back.

Without thinking, she swung her legs out over the edge of the sofa, looking straight into the dark pools of his eyes so he knew she was sincere—because she *was*.

'Why would I want to lose one of the best friends I've had since I moved here?' She smiled a little shyly at him. 'And anyway—you'll have met the woman of your dreams pretty soon and, hard as it is to believe, she might actually want you to herself. Though I'm sure that'll wear off with time. And when it does you can both have me over for dinner—I'll even bring the wine...'

Somehow she managed to hold her smile, but it hadn't been easy. Because she knew the relationship they had would change if they both had partners. What she hadn't known was how much the idea of it would hurt. They'd never be the same again, would they?

A part of her wanted things to stay the same.

Quinn continued staring at her across the divide. 'She's gonna have to be something pretty darn special to pin me down. You know that, don't you?'

'I wouldn't let you settle for anything else, would I?' She lifted her brows in question.

'Not even to win the bet?'

'Not even to win the bet.'

'Promise?'

It was the huskier-than-usual edge to his rough voice that did it. Clare's subconscious was taking it as a sign of vulnerability. And in a man like Quinn it was so potent she felt herself drawn to her feet and tugged towards the windows—the need to reassure him was as vital as the need for air. When she was standing on the other side of the glass she smiled, hoping he understood how much she wanted to see him happy.

'Cross my heart.'

When she lifted a hand to back up the pledge she knew she'd made a mistake. Because with the open invitation he immediately lowered his gaze to her breasts, where it lingered long enough for her to feel as if she'd been touched. She watched the rise and fall of his chest change rhythm, her own breathing matching the faster pace. And then she saw his gaze slide lower still: over her bare midriff, down the legs she'd always thought were too skinny and all the way to the tips of her toes—the toes it took every ounce of control she possessed to stop from curling into the wooden floor.

With a sharp upward jerk of his chin his gaze tangled with hers, making her irresponsible heart kick up against her ribcage before he frowned—as if he wasn't any happier with what he'd just done than she was that she'd invited it to happen.

'Should have pulled the drapes…'

'I wasn't expecting company.' Clare dug her fingernails into the soft flesh of her palm to stop any attempt at covering up when the damage was already done. 'Just as well it's only you, really…'

'Many things I may be. Blind isn't one of them.'

Her jaw dropped.

But before she could think of anything coherent to say Quinn pushed to his feet and turned away, looking over his shoulder to add, 'We'll have the dating talk in the office.'

'Okay.'

'And pull the drapes.'

Her hands lifted to do as she was bid while she watched him make short work of the steps with his long legs. And when the curtains were closed she kept her hands gripped tight to the edges, while she took long, deep breaths to bring her heart-rate back into a normal rhythm. She felt as if she'd just run a marathon.

*And he'd done that just by looking at her?* No wonder women fell all over him!

It was because it was the first time he'd ever looked at her the way a man looked at a woman, that was all. Up till then she'd been—well—she'd just *been there* as far as he was concerned.

Thing was, she wasn't entirely sure she wanted to be in the background to him. Not that she wanted anything more, but she didn't want to be invisible either. There were times when it was all too easy to feel that way in a city the size of New York—especially for someone who came from a tiny village in the west of Ireland where everyone knew everyone.

If a connoisseur of women like Quinn Cassidy couldn't see her then what hope did she have of not disappearing into the crowd? And she *wanted* to be seen. The thought surprised her, but it shouldn't have. Not really. It was time. She was long since over the mistake she'd made; it was time to move on—to get back in the game as Quinn had said. And if he was ready to make a commitment to someone then surely she could give love another try too? She'd just have to make sure she didn't pick someone who was a womanizer this time round—been there, done that. If she hadn't, then she might have been tempted to try some of that flirting with Quinn she'd wondered about. And that?

Well, that was a disaster waiting to happen.

## CHAPTER FOUR

'HAS O'CONNOR TALKED to Madison about any plans she's been making?' Quinn casually bounced the basketball from one hand to the other, bending at the knee and raising an arm above his head before gauging the distance, pushing off the balls of his feet, and sinking it through the hoop.

He'd been sinking hoops with Morgan and Evan at the court a couple of blocks from where he now lived since they'd been tall enough to stand a chance of scoring points. And while he was avoiding Clare's dumb talk on dating etiquette he'd felt the need for some male bonding—even if it meant broaching the subject of her in front of the new guy who had joined their team.

Jamie had been the original fourth member of their crew, but after his run-in with Quinn there was no question of him ever returning without a replay of their last talk. It didn't stop Quinn's resentment of anyone new taking his place though…

'The matchmaking thing, you mean?' Morgan got the ball before it hit the ground. 'How's that panning out for you? You registered for a dinner service yet?'

'Funny.'

'You better win this one.' Evan slapped Quinn's back hard enough to rock him forwards. 'My money's on you—don't let me down.'

'There's no way she's pinning me down—I'd have found the right woman on my own by now if she existed—it's a percentages thing.' It wasn't his fault he'd never met a woman he wanted to keep around for long. And anyway, he was a busy man—women had a tendency to expect a guy to commit to more time at a certain point in the relationship.

If Clare left he'd be even busier. Not to mention on edge and tense in a way he hadn't been in two years. With her there he'd been calmer, more relaxed, less likely to suffer an ulcer by pushing himself too hard when there wasn't as much of a need to succeed as there had once been. Going back to the kind of life he'd had before Clare was less and less appealing the more time he had to think about it…

He set his hands on his hips, watching for an opportunity to steal the basketball back. 'I take it she hasn't talked about quitting work and moving out, then?'

The bouncing stopped and a huddle formed around him. Morgan was the first to ask 'Since when?'

Evan followed, in the traditional pecking order. 'She heading back to Ireland?'

'O'Connor? That's the cute redhead, right?'

Quinn glared at the new guy as he dared to join the conversation. Since when did he think he had the right to join a discussion on Quinn's private life? But Morgan was already getting down to details.

'What makes you think she's leaving?'

After another five seconds of glaring to make his

point, Quinn turned his attention to Morgan. 'Maybe when she said so. I'm intuitive that way.'

'Oh, this is really bugging you, isn't it?'

Quinn shrugged, lifting his forearm to swipe it across his damp forehead while he fought off another wave of anger for coming on to her the way he had. 'I thought she might have said something to one of the other girls.'

Evan's dark eyes sparkled in a knowing way that merited a *don't go there* glare from Quinn, to which he responded with his trademark surrender hands.

'I'm just saying—'

'Well, don't.'

The new guy tried again. 'I didn't know you two were a couple.'

Morgan smiled. 'Oh, they're not a couple in the traditional sense of the word…'

Quinn snatched the ball out from under his elbow. 'I can afford to go join a country club somewhere, you know. I don't have to mess about on this court with you losers any more.'

'Yeah, but this is *our* court. You don't ever forget where you came from—remember?'

Evan nodded. 'Nowhere's better than Brooklyn.'

When they high fived each other while still looking at him, Quinn shook his head. An investment consultant, a cop-turned-security-specialist and a big-shot club owner, they'd all come a long way from their early days. But when they got together with any shape of a ball they still had an innate ability to act like teenagers. There was probably a reason women believed men never grew up. What they didn't get was that the responsibilities that came with age and hard-earned money meant there was an even greater need for time spent messing around with a ball.

But it wasn't helping Quinn.

If Clare had been talking to the other women about her plans to go it alone then he'd know she was further down the line. If she hadn't then he'd know it was a new idea, which meant he had time to—

Well, he'd get to that part when he had the information he needed. All he knew was that it wasn't just about work any more. Her running hotfoot out of every corner of his life felt distinctly *personal.*

So he asked the one question that had been eating at him most. 'Does she know about Jamie?'

'You have another girl?'

Quinn's head turned so fast towards the new guy he heard the bones in his neck crack. 'Look—I know you're just here to shoot hoops, and I'm sure deep down you're a great guy, but take five, would you? Go get some iced water or something…'

The commanding tone to his voice was all it took.

When the younger man shrugged and turned away, Morgan lifted and dropped an arm. 'Is there any chance of you not scaring off another one? I'm running out of second cousins.'

Quinn pushed again. 'Does she know?'

'I don't see why you don't just tell her. You stood up for her when you barely knew her—she was nothing to you back then.' He threw in a smile of encouragement. 'She might be grateful you did it.'

'Before or after she works out I made things worse?'

Morgan grimaced.

And Quinn had his answer. 'So she doesn't know.'

'The only way she'd know was if one of us told her.'

Evan placed a hand on his shoulder, squeezing hard before he let go. 'It's always been your call.'

Quinn nodded brusquely, turning his head and letting his gaze travel to the wire surrounding the court and the traffic beyond as a walking tour made its way past, a guide's voice telling loud tales of the Brooklyn they'd all known most of their lives—even if Quinn had arrived a little later than the others.

'If she was planning on going home to Ireland we'd all have heard about it by now,' Morgan added.

Quinn mumbled the words 'This is her home now. She belongs here.'

There was a long enough silence to draw his attention back to their faces, each of them studying him closely enough to make him feel like a bug under a microscope. 'What?'

'Nothing…'

'Nope. Me either.'

'Well, let's finish the game, then—I'm at the Manhattan Club in a couple of hours.' This was his last respite before he had to take his genius plan to stage two—the plan that had seemed like such a great idea before he'd taken a good long look at Clare in what had barely made it past the quota of material needed for a swimsuit.

For coming up on eighteen months he'd managed to avoid looking at her that closely. *Eighteen months.* And now it was indelibly burned into his brain so he knew he'd never be able to look at her without seeing her as more than Clare who lived downstairs and worked for him.

Tearing up the court like a man possessed, he threw all his anger and frustration into the physicality of the game, ignoring the heavy heat magnified several degrees by a concrete cocoon of tall buildings around him and under his feet.

Why couldn't she have been wearing sweats two sizes too big? He didn't want to see her as a woman. The second he started looking at her that way it changed things. And he knew himself. If she didn't see him as a man in return it would become some kind of challenge to him, wouldn't it?

And then she'd be in *real* trouble.

Clare stared with wide eyes at her own reflection.

'You look amazing, Friday.'

*Not* the word she'd have used. 'It's too short.'

When she tugged on the hem in a vain attempt to make it longer the younger woman laughed, meeting her gaze in the mirror. 'Not with those supermodel legs it's not. Hostesses represent that kind of glamour, even if we're just glorified waitresses. We're the first thing people see when they walk in the VIP lounge. Think of us as business class air stewardesses, or Miss United States contestants. You could do this job, you know, when you get bored looking at the boss every day…'

*Looking at him?* Oh, chance would be a fine thing. He'd been the Scarlet Pimpernel for the last forty-eight hours and she'd sought him here and sought him there while he'd deftly managed to find one reason after another to stay out of the office.

She tugged on the hem of the shimmering black dress again, trying to convince herself it was only her toothpick legs on show and that in the modern age legs weren't anywhere near scandalous. It could have been much worse, all things considered. But she wouldn't have done this kind of job unless they were really, *really* stuck—cute wasn't anywhere in the same region as glamorous, was it?

Her gaze lifted to her tumble of red curls framing a face so unfamiliar to her, with huge, darkly made up eyes designed to look sultry and full lips shining a bright enough dusky rose to make it look as if she was permanently ready to be kissed.

Well, she'd wanted people to see her, hadn't she?

'Come on, I'll show you the basics and we'll practise the patented smile and walking in those heels.'

Clare grimaced. 'Terrific.'

'You'll be great, Friday—you always are—it's why we all love you so much: you're a trooper.'

Yup, everyone who worked for Quinn Cassidy adored her—barring the man himself, who apparently couldn't bear to stand in the same room as her. If he wanted out of the stupid bet then all he had to do was say so. She didn't have a problem with that.

What she *did* have a problem with was how much she'd missed having him around. She'd missed his gruff voice, his lazy smile, the way he had of occupying her time with attempting to keep him in line work-wise, the number of times in a day he made her laugh…Not that she was likely to tell him any of that when he already had an ego the size of Manhattan.

But it didn't bode well for the long term if she missed him before their relationship had been changed with the arrival of new partners…

Well, maybe she wasn't as independent as she'd thought she was. It was a depressing thought.

By the time Quinn had showered, changed, and made it back into the city, the club had filled to capacity with members from their exclusive guest list. So he checked there hadn't been any major hiccups anywhere before stepping into his usual role. It was a few hours in, when he was halfway round the VIP lounge making sure the more famous of the faces were being pandered to, that he did a double take.

A blinding rage swiftly followed.

With a forced smile for the A-List actor who'd had his arm around Clare's waist, he closed his fingers firmly round her elbow and guided her forcefully through the crowd into a deserted hallway, where the music was lower.

'What do you think you're doing?'

Clare twisted her elbow free, rubbing at it while she frowned up at him. 'I'm sorry—it's been so long since I last saw you I didn't recognize you in there.'

'I could say the same—why are you wearing that?' To his complete and utter fury he let his gaze slide over her again, what he could see making him stifle a groan of frustration. It was like some kind of test. He'd meant it when he'd told her he wasn't *blind*!

It wasn't as if he didn't see at least a dozen women wearing short dresses coated in overlapping onyx discs a minimum of three nights a week. He'd seen so many he barely looked any more—but then none of those women had been Clare, had they?

Clare wearing one was something entirely different.

What was with his obsession with her legs all of a sudden anyway? He'd seen them hundreds of times. Granted, it had never been when they were encased in sheer black stockings with their shape enhanced the way only dangerously high heels could.

His gaze rose.

The hair and make-up were something new too—new and completely unnecessary. Clare didn't need that much stuff on her face, or her hair curled. He'd always liked the way her hair framed her face in soft waves and the fresh, natural—

He gritted his teeth. *'Go home, Clare.'*

Moist lips parted in surprise a split second before he saw fire spark in her eyes. 'I'm not being sent home like some kind of rebellious teenager. We're three down with flu on a night this place is packed to the gills. What is your *problem*?'

'You don't belong in here!'

Raising his voice proved a bad move on his behalf, simply fuelling the fire. 'I've worked behind the bar here at least a half dozen times!'

'*Behind* the bar! Not on the main floor with Hollywood actors coming on to you and trying to get your phone number.'

'Well, *excuse me*, but who was it told me to *get back in the game*? You can't have it both ways—make up your mind, Quinn.' She shook her head, curls bobbing against her bare shoulders. 'I'm going back to work.'

'This isn't your job.' He blocked her escape, anger still bubbling inside him like boiling water. And he couldn't remember the last time he'd been so angry.

That was a lie—he could remember the exact time and place—and the fact that it had indirectly involved her that time too.

'I'm not kidding—you're not going back in there. Get changed and go home. I'll get one of the limo drivers to take you.'

For a heartbeat he thought he'd got through to her. But then she took two steps back and lifted her chin, her eyes sparkling as she held her arms out to her sides. And when she spoke her voice was thready with what he assumed was suppressed anger.

'If you think I'm not up to the glamorous standard you expect in the VIP room then just say so, because—'

She thought she wasn't gorgeous enough to work alongside the other girls? It was precisely *because* she was gorgeous that he didn't want her there. It was the very fact his eyes had been all too recently opened to how sexy she could look in or out of that short, little dress.

With considerable effort he managed to stop himself swearing. 'It's got nothing to do with how you look. You don't work in there.'

'I work for *you*!' She dropped her hands to her hips and scowled hard. 'And working for you means filling in wherever we're short—you know that—so why is it suddenly such a big deal this time?'

Because it was. That was why. But it was hardly the most mature answer. And, yes, he knew he was being unreasonable—date/don't date—keep working for him even if he had to trick her into it/don't let her do the job she'd always done…

She was making him crazy.

'If I have to carry you out of here over my shoulder you know I'll do it.'

Clare chewed on her lower lip, then damped it with the rosy tip of her tongue, drawing his gaze and increasing his frown. Then she took a deep breath and focused on his jawline.

'If you want me to leave you'll have to fire me. I don't think I want to work for you any more anyway. Not when you're being like this.'

When her lower lip trembled before she caught it between her teeth Quinn dropped his chin to his chest and took several calming breaths, puffing his cheeks out as he exhaled while his heart thundered as hard as it had during his session on the basketball court. And naturally Clare chose that moment to step in close enough for the light scent of springtime flowers to tease his nostrils.

Closing his eyes for a brief moment, he breathed deep and then looked up without lifting his chin. 'I'm not firing you. I just need you to go home. Please.'

*Please* had to help, right? Desperate times and all that—and it was for her own good. If she kept wandering under his nose pointing out how sexy she could be then there was going to come a time when he wouldn't be held responsible for his own actions.

She shook her head, her eyes shimmering as she asked in a tremulous voice, 'What's happened to us lately?'

Now, there was a question. One he wished he had an answer for. Because *something* had changed. The equilibrium was gone—and whatever it was had him in the kind of free fall he had absolutely no experience of.

Until he'd sorted through just what was making him act the way he was, he couldn't keep taking it out on Clare, could he?

He lifted his head. 'You don't belong somewhere partygoers might paw you after a few drinks. The girls who work that room know how to deal with them—they're tough cookies.'

'You still see me as some pathetic female in need of rescuing? Great—it's good to know I've come so far in the last year.'

'You're not a pathetic female.'

'You're treating me like I am.'

'No, what I'm doing is looking out for you. I'm told it's what friends do.'

She tilted her chin up the way she always did when

she was drawing on her inner strength. 'I'm not your responsibility, Quinn.'

'In here you are—my club, my rules. And if I say you're going home, then you're going home.'

For a second she gaped at him. Then her hands rose to her hips again. Her head was cocked at an angle, and sparks danced in her eyes just before they narrowed…

Heaven help him—he'd never been so tempted to kiss an unreceptive woman in all his born days.

But before he did something incredibly stupid, and before she let loose, he lowered his voice to the deathly calm, deliberately slow tone that signalled he'd reached the end of his rope.

'Walking out or being carried out?'

'You wouldn't *dare*—'

'Your choice.' He bent over at the waist, grabbed her hand in a vice-like grip—and tossed her over his shoulder, turning swiftly on his heel.

'Quinn Cassidy, you put me down this minute or—'

When she struggled he lifted his free hand and reached for a hold to steady her, his fingers curling above her knee. She gasped, stilled, and Quinn felt the impact of what he'd done clean to the soles of his feet.

The silken material of her stockings seemed to crackle against the tips of his fingers. And he couldn't stop it happening, errant fingers sampling the softness of the material and the heated skin underneath. Would her skin be as soft if he touched it without the minute covering, or even softer? There had always been something incredibly enticing about the sensitive skin behind a woman's knees, or inside her elbows, or in the hollow where her neck met her shoulders, or on her inside leg further up—

Quinn's stride faltered as he felt the most basic of male responses slamming into him uninvited. And as a result he had to grit his teeth so hard to regain some semblance of control that his jaw ached from the effort.

'If that hand goes so much as one millimetre higher I'm going to scream harassment so loud your mother will hear me in Brooklyn.'

'What hand?' He lengthened his stride.

Clare grasped hold of fistfuls of his jacket as he jogged down the stairs. 'And if people can see my underwear—'

Glancing sideways, he scowled at the lacy upper edge of stocking he could see, swearing beneath his breath.

'I told you to leave. *You* wouldn't listen.'

'You are the most ill-tempered, unreasonable, stubborn—'

'I've been called worse than that in my time, sweetheart—trust me.' Kicking the toe of his shoe on the bottom of the front doors he dumped her on her feet in front of one of the club's massive security guards. 'Get Clare a limo. She's going home.'

'Feel sick, Friday?'

Clare lifted her hands to push her curls off her flushed cheeks, grumbling beneath her breath. 'To the pit of my stomach, Leroy.'

When he went to call a limo forward Quinn spread his feet and crossed his arms, forming a human barrier over the swinging doors. He watched while Clare tugged angrily on the hem of her skirt.

'I hate you when you get like this.'

'I said please.'

'You said please as a last-ditch effort and we both

know it.' She blew an angry puff of air at a curl of hair, folding her arms to match his. 'You are *not* a nice person.'

Quinn shrugged. 'Never claimed to be.'

'Has it ever occurred to you the reason you have so few friends is because you can be like this?'

It was out of his mouth before he knew his brain had formed the words: 'Has it ever occurred to you I have so few friends because I like it that way?'

When the obvious questions formed in her eyes he turned his profile to her. May as well just throw his entire life story at her and have done. It was cheaper than therapy, right?

'Why?' Her voice had changed.

From his peripheral vision he saw her take a step forward, his spine immediately straightened in response. Enough was enough. 'I'll bring your things back with me. Just go home, Clare. I don't want you in there dressed like that. End of story.' He turned his head and fixed her gaze with a steady stare. 'Just this one time do me a favour—and don't push me.'

When he saw the limo pull up behind her he jerked his chin at it. 'Go.'

He turned and had his palm on the door when he heard her low voice behind him. The emotion he could hear crushed the air from his chest.

'I don't want to go back to the way we were before we became friends…'

Quinn felt the same way—but rather than saying so he pushed the door open and walked away. If she'd been anyone else—*anyone*—he'd have acted on how she was making him feel. He'd have found an outlet for all his frustration. But she was Clare. She was *Clare*, damn it—and she mattered to him. The fact he'd reached out a helping hand when she needed it in the past may have been partly because he felt bad about the tangled web of lies woven around her not long after she came to the States. But she mattered to him now.

Maybe more than she should.

## CHAPTER FIVE

'CAN WE TRY AGAIN?'

Clare didn't get it. This was the third woman in a row Quinn hadn't got past a first date with. What the heck was he doing wrong? Because if he was doing it on purpose…

She tried to get to the root of the problem. 'Can I ask exactly what it was that put you off going on a second date with him?'

It was the kind of question she always asked so she could build up a better profile of her clients. Maybe a little more than professional curiosity on this occasion, but still…

'It'll help me with your next match if I know…'

There was a pause. 'Don't get me wrong—I mean, he was charming and attentive and all that. And there's no doubting he's incredibly good looking. But…'

'But?'

'Well, it took me a while to figure it out, cos he was clever about letting me talk about myself. And, let's face it, we like it when they're interested in what we have to say. But when I tried getting to know *him…*'

Ahhh—now, *that* she got. It had taken spending practically every hour of every day with Quinn before Clare had had a chance to get to know him better. Prior to that he'd been a constant brooding presence in the background. Everyone else had made her feel welcome from the day she'd arrived, but Quinn…

'Thanks for telling me, Jayne. I'll call you in a few days, when I've had a chance to look through your match list again.'

'Actually I was wondering about maybe seeing Adam again…'

Clare smiled. 'I think Adam would like that. I'll talk to him and get back to you.'

Her gaze slid to the glass doors as she hung up. Quinn's dark head was bowed as he flipped through the mail.

'Congratulations. You're three for three.'

'Hmmm?' He didn't lift his head.

'That was Jayne. You want to tell me what was wrong with this one?'

When he glanced briefly her way she smiled, ignoring the way her pulse skipped out of its regular rhythm. Not that she wanted to put it down to nervousness, but things had been different since the night he'd carried her out of the club. And she knew she couldn't blame it all on the fact that they'd argued either…

She had watched him that night. It wasn't as if she hadn't seen him working the floor on the odd nights she'd stood in, but she'd never paid as much attention before. And in the VIP lounge, between all the smiling and accepting tips from customers, she'd been more than a little impressed by what she'd seen.

She'd always assumed he'd gone into the club business because he loved the constant party atmosphere—and there was certainly no disputing that he'd laughed loud and often. But he hadn't partied alongside the guests, hadn't touched a single drop of alcohol, and he'd had a quiet hold on the room that had been positively palpable. He'd noticed everything—down to the tiniest, seemingly insignificant detail; the merest hint of a voice rising and he had been there to defuse the problem with a hundred-watt smile and a good dose of patented Cassidy wit. He'd greeted everyone, no matter how internationally famous or infamous, as if they had been long-lost family members, nearly all of them returning the courtesy by making sure they'd seen him to shake his hand or kiss his cheek before they left…

And in a dark designer label suit he hadn't been just sexy as all get out, he'd been imposingly in charge. It was *business* to him—and a firm reminder to Clare never to make assumptions about him ever again.

'She was high maintainence.'

When he headed for his office, Clare pushed her chair back and followed him. 'In what way?'

Tossing the mail on his desk, he shrugged his shoulders out of his jacket, hanging it on a rack in the corner before glancing at her. 'In every way. Did nothing but talk about herself all night, for starters…'

Clare quirked a brow. 'Really? That's funny—she says you encouraged her to do that to avoid answering questions about yourself.'

When he began to roll up the sleeves of his pale blue shirt, Clare's gaze dropped to watch the movement of his long fingers. A flex of his forearm muscle and the stilling of his hand jerked her gaze back up.

He was studying her with hooded eyes and lazy blinks of thick lashes. He looked away and swapped arms. 'She picked at every course, complained four times to the waiter, name-dropped for all she was worth and spent a half-hour talking to me about the best beauty treatments in her favourite spa—*high maintainence.*'

Clare leaned her shoulder against the doorjamb. 'The last one was no good because "she barely talked, ate too much and dressed like a Quaker." Quote, unquote.'

'And?'

When he smoothed his hand up to push the folded sleeve into place she found her gaze dropping again, convinced she could hear the sound of his skin brushing over the light dusting of hair on his forearm.

*'O'Connor?'* The edge to his gravelly voice brought her gaze back up again. 'Could we get to the point?'

Impatient. He'd been that way more and more of late. And he'd just seen her watching him, hadn't he? There was no way he hadn't. Judging by the tic that had developed on one side of his strong jaw, he wasn't best pleased about it either.

It was the third time he'd made her shrivel up inside with embarrassment. First when she'd inadvertently invited him to look at her semi-naked body, then when he'd made it plain she wasn't up to the standard expected of hostesses in the VIP room, and now because she'd just given away the fact that she was noticing him physically.

But then the latter had been creeping up on her of late; she still hadn't quite got round to hiding it. It was because she was matchmaking for him, at least she hoped it was—couldn't be anything more. She wouldn't *let it* be anything more.

Slowly damping her lower lip, she smoothed both

lips together, as if evening out lipstick, before lifting her chin. 'If you're going to dismiss all of them after one date, maybe I should just let you see some of the files before I set up any more.'

That was something she never did normally, because allowing someone to judge someone else on looks alone was one of the major mistakes people all made before they came to her. Something she'd once done herself.

He took a breath that widened his broad chest and it took every ounce of self-control she had not to drop her gaze again to watch the movement.

Quinn shrugged. 'It might speed things up some.'

Silently she vowed she was never matchmaking for someone close to her again. It took too much out of her. Though she somehow doubted she'd have fretted as much if it had been Morgan or Evan.

The silent confession made her frown.

Quinn lifted an arm and checked his heavy watch. 'Bring 'em in now, if you like. I have ten minutes.'

Ten minutes to select someone he might end up spending the rest of his life with?

She turned on her heel and marched to her desk, muttering below her breath. 'Taking this seriously, my eye. He spends more time selecting people for his flipping VIP list than he does with someone he might wake up with every morning. God help her. She'll be wielding an axe after less than six months—'

He called after her from the other room. 'You need to speak up if I'm s'posed to hear that.'

Clare closed her eyes and quietly called him a name.

When she dumped all his matches on the desk in front of him he rolled back his chair and reached out a long leg to toe another chair forward.

'Sit.'

Her brows rose; the vaguest hint of a smile toyed with the corners of Quinn's mouth before he turned his attention to the first file.

'Nope.'

Clare reluctantly sat down as he lifted another file and began reading. And since she had nothing better to do she decided to study his profile to see what else she might have missed.

Her examination started with his close-cropped midnight-black hair, down over the equally dark brows folded downwards as he concentrated on the file. It lingered on the flicker of thick lashes framing his amazingly blue eyes, and then she smiled at the way his nose twitched the tiniest amount a second before he glanced her way. Almost as if he could sniff out her unusual levels of curiosity.

'How long are you gonna stay annoyed about what happened at the club?' He tossed the file.

Clare rolled her chair closer, glancing down at the photograph on the next file before he discarded it. 'Who says I'm still annoyed? And what was wrong with that one, exactly?'

'Dated her last year.' He studied the fourth one with a little more interest. 'And you're still annoyed—I could cut the atmosphere in this office with a knife.'

'Oh, and that's entirely my fault, is it? What's wrong with *her*?'

'Dated that one too. I'm just trying to remember what it was that bugged me about her.'

He nodded, tossing it to one side with the others. 'Now I remember. Has a million cats.'

Clare rolled closer still, his scent wrapping around her like a blanket. '*Three* cats.'

'In a tiny one-bedroom apartment. And they slept on the bed.'

Yes, obviously he'd know that, wouldn't he? She took a deep breath of his scent and rolled back a little when she realized he was about to discard the next one. She'd forgotten she'd offered to find matches for a few girls after tearful post-Tiffany-box phone calls, but she remembered the one he was looking at now.

'Go ahead and lose that one too. She spent a half hour calling you names when you dumped her.'

'Built your business on my cast-offs, did you?'

No. She could probably double her client list if she did. 'I knew I shouldn't have let you skip the dating talk.'

'So why did you?'

Because having felt his hands on her when he'd carried her, she hadn't wanted to chance getting details to go with the images born of her furtive imagination, that was why.

She sighed heavily when another file bit the dust. 'What's wrong with that one? She's stunning.'

'Redhead.'

Clare fought the urge to tuck a strand of red hair behind her ear, her voice sharp. 'Maybe you should just tell me what it is you're looking for.'

'Maybe you should tell me why it is you're still so mad about that night at the club.'

'The fact that you hauled me out of there, tossed me over your shoulder and sent me home with my tail between my legs isn't enough?' To say nothing of the fact she'd made an idiot of herself by saying what she had before he'd walked away. Would it have killed him to say something in reply?

'I said please.'

'Yes, I remember. But I never really had a choice, did I? And I hate to tell you, but these bullying tactics of yours need to stop. They're not remotely attractive in my opinion.'

His hand hovered over the next file and then dropped while he slowly turned his chair towards her. 'So what *is*, then—in your opinion?'

He wanted a list? She was supposed to just sit there, with his knee scant inches from hers and the vivid blue of his sensational eyes studying her face so intently, and tell him what she found attractive about him? Had the air conditioning gone down? Lord, it was warm.

She fought the need to flap a hand in front of her face. The cotton of her blouse was sticking to her back so she was forced to lean forwards, away from the heated leather of the chair.

Which Quinn apparently took as an invitation to lean forwards too, so that when Clare's gaze lifted his face was a little too close for comfort.

Her breath hitched.

And Quinn's washed over the tip of her nose as he spoke. 'Go on, then. I'm all ears.'

Clare tried to find general answers to his question rather than personal ones. Not an easy task with her brain wrapped in cotton wool. And when the portion of it still working was finding so many of the answers straight in front of her eyes: the sinful sweep of that mouth, the one narrow lock of short hair just long enough to brush against his forehead. How could she possibly be attracted to him *now*, when he was being a jerk? Instead of before, when he'd made her smile every day and she'd loved spending time with him?

Her tongue stuck to the roof of her mouth.

Quinn's gaze shifted, the blue of his eyes darkening a shade while he examined a wave of hair framing one side of her face. And when Clare saw his fingers flex against the files she wondered if he'd considered brushing it back for her. A part of her ached when he didn't…

'Well?'

'It's…well…it's subjective, isn't it?'

'All right.' His gaze locked with hers again. 'Tell me what it was you found so attractive about Jamie, then.'

Clare's eyes widened. No way was she having that discussion with Quinn. *No way.*

Apparently he knew her well enough to see that, because he nodded brusquely and changed tactic. 'You still hung up on him? Is that why you're not dating?'

Where on earth had *that* come from? Surely he knew the answer? There were days when she couldn't even remember what it was that had made her throw caution to the wind in the first place, defying good advice from family and friends who'd worried that if she got into trouble so far from home they wouldn't be close enough to help. Justifiably worried, as it had turned out in the end…

But it had taken the all-consuming misery of complete humiliation for her to know she'd probably never loved Jamie the way she should have. She'd just been swept away by the romance and the adventure of it all. And it hadn't been enough. If he'd been right for her she would never have felt the niggling doubt in the back of her head that had been there even when she'd said yes to his proposal…

So she could answer Quinn's question with complete conviction. 'No, he has nothing to do with it.'

'Do I remind you of him?'

Clare gaped at him. *What?* But she could tell from the determined fix of his jaw that Quinn wasn't messing with her; he needed to know. Though why he would even think it in the first place astounded her.

'You're nothing like him.'

All right that wasn't a completely honest answer, and judging by the look on Quinn's face he knew it too, so she silently cleared her throat to say the rest more firmly. 'You use the same phrases sometimes and you have the same accent—but so do Evan and Morgan. The only reason you're like that is because you all grew up together.'

'And that's it?'

His voice was even rougher than usual, and a harsh cramp crushed the air out of her chest so that she exhaled her answer. 'Yes.'

And, with her all too recent revelations on the subject of how little she really knew him, it was reassuring to know there were still some things she knew with her whole heart. Quinn might be a serial-dater but at least he was open about it. He didn't pretend to be someone he wasn't. Forewarned was forearmed. And any woman who fell for him fell for him faults and all. He would never let her be made a fool of the way Jamie had.

Quinn Cassidy had an honourable streak a mile wide, despite the matching streak of wicked sensuality.

He studied her some more—as if he needed to find visual confirmation in her eyes. Then—Lord help her—his gaze dropped briefly to her mouth. And Clare couldn't even manage an inward breath to ease her aching chest until he looked back into her eyes.

'So you're not dating because you're afraid of getting hurt again? Is that it?'

'No. I'm not dating because I—'

'Don't have time?' His mouth twisted into a cruel impersonation of humour. 'Yes, you tried that one already. And it's part of the reason I'm putting a stop to all the extra shifts you put in at the clubs. I've told them you'll not be filling in any more.'

Clare opened her mouth.

But Quinn kept going. 'It's not like you're not being asked out on dates either, is it? Mitch has been flirting with you for months now.'

When he frowned, Clare's eyes widened in amazement, because for a second it almost looked as if he was—*jealous*? Was that why he hadn't wanted her in the club that night? Had the thought of men coming on to her bothered him?

As if able to read the thoughts in her eyes, Quinn frowned harder and turned towards his desk, leaving her looking at the tic that had returned to his jaw. 'Next time he asks you out you should say yes. You gotta start somewhere.'

So much for jealousy; a jealous man didn't send the woman he was interested in out on a date with another guy, did he?

'No one high maintainence, no cat ladies and *definitely* no exes from here on in.' Gathering the files into one pile again, he set them on the edge of his desk.

And if he was remotely interested in her as anything other than a friend he would hardly continue dating under her nose, would he? Clare reached for the files, angry with herself for momentarily feeling pleased he might have been jealous.

'Can she breathe in and out?'

'Take that as a prerequisite.'

'You know you can still back out of this any time you want.' Clare took a deep breath as she prepared to push to her feet. 'Just say the word and I'll start planning my matchmaking nights at your clubs.'

Reaching for a padded envelope on the top of the pile of mail, Quinn grumbled back, 'Would I still be wading my way through them if I wanted to quit?'

'So you're not messing up the dates on purpose?'

'Why would I do that?'

'You tell me.'

'I may twist the rules but I've never shied away from playing the game—have I?'

The phone began to ring on her desk, and Quinn glanced sideways at her when she didn't move. 'It's traditional to answer it when it makes that noise.'

Clare stared at him for a long moment. But she never could leave a phone ringing—even if it was a public phone box somewhere. So, pursing her lips in annoyance, she pushed to her feet and walked into the reception area, wracking her brain for reasons why she'd used to enjoy Quinn's company…

'Cassidy Group.'

'Hi, gorgeous. How you doing?'

'Mitch.' Clare smiled when she saw Quinn look towards the open doorway. 'All the better for hearing your voice—as always.'

He chuckled. 'Ready to go out with me yet?'

It was the same conversation they'd been having every week for months. But with Quinn frowning Clare smiled and changed her usual answer. *'I'd love to.'*

Quinn sharply pushed his chair back and took two

long strides forward to swing his door shut. It slammed. And Clare smiled all the more.

'So, where are you taking me?'

# CHAPTER SIX

QUINN LEANED BACK IN his chair, dropping his hands below the table, where they formed fists against his thighs. It was as visceral a reaction as he'd ever experienced and, realistically, he had no one to blame but himself. But telling her to go out on a date was one thing. Listening to her accept Mitch over the phone was another. *Seeing them together...* Well...if he'd taken a second to think about how that might feel he might have been better prepared.

'Quinn?'

He forced a smile for the woman across the table from him. Under normal circumstances he'd have been pretty pleased with date number four. Blonde, gorgeous, bright, funny, easy-going... The kind of woman he'd have asked out if he'd met her on his own. But he'd known inside fifteen minutes that there was no spark.

His errant gaze sought Clare again as she walked through the room with that damned feminine grace of hers. No legs on display, but she was sensational regardless, the material of her long skirt flowing like liquid silk with each step. Had she known where he was taking his date for dinner? There was no way she could have. And

Mitch was obviously out to impress if he was paying for dinner in the Venetian Renaissance-style dining room at Daniel.

She had her hair up in one of those ultra-feminine styles that made a man's fingers itch to let it loose. And when she leaned her head to one side to listen to what Mitch said as he drew out her chair a long earring brushed against her neck. Her eyes sparkled, she laughed musically…

Quinn fought a deep-seated urge to storm over and remove her from the room the same way he had from his club.

'Is that Clare?'

He dragged his gaze away. 'Yes.'

Lorie's eyes lit up. 'Is that her boyfriend?'

A part of him wanted to yell *no* good and loud, but he swallowed the word. 'You work at the Natural History Museum? What do you do there?'

While Lorie talked he forced himself to stay focused on her. Being a course ahead of Clare and Mitch was a bonus—all he had to do was concentrate through dessert and they were out of there.

When the waiter laid the napkin across her lap Clare smiled up at him and accepted the menu. She knew Mitch was making a real effort and she appreciated that—she did. He was a genuinely nice guy. It was just a shame that every time she looked into his brown eyes she found herself wishing they were blue.

She lifted her water and took a sip, glancing over the rim at the other tables as she swallowed.

The water went down the wrong way.

Mitch chuckled as she grasped for her napkin, choking behind it as tears came to her eyes. 'You okay?'

'Mmm-hmm.' She managed to surface for a weak smile.

Someone, somewhere, really had it in for her, didn't they? She coughed again, waving a limp hand at him. 'Went down the wrong way.'

'I guessed.'

Her chest ached. And she could try telling herself it was due to the coughing, but that would be a big fat lie. Had Quinn known where Mitch was taking her for dinner? If he had she was going to kill him…

'This place is lovely,' she managed in a strangled voice she hoped Mitch would put down to the choking.

'It is, isn't it?'

Smoothing the napkin back into place on her lap, she lifted the menu and tried her best to study it. After three attempts she gave in and peeked over the edge to look across the room again. Well, at least it looked as if Quinn was getting on better with this date than he had on the others—that was something. She frowned.

Mitch smiled. 'Do you know what you want?'

Now, there was a question. Clare smiled back, and then forced her gaze to the menu. She could do this. She could pretend Quinn wasn't across the room from her—on a date she'd set up for him—she just needed to concentrate

'So, Mitch, have you always been a wine merchant?'

Lorie dropped out of Quinn's favour the second she decided to start eating off his plate. He hated women who did that. If they'd wanted what he was eating then they should have ordered it in the first place as far as he was concerned. And it didn't help that when he glanced at Clare she was feeding Mitch something off her fork, one hand cupped beneath it in case anything dropped while she watched him lean forward to accept the offering.

Quinn lifted his napkin and tossed it to one side of his plate while he fought the need to growl. Was she playing up to Mitch on purpose because she knew he was there?

Although she hadn't given any indication she'd even seen him, had she? Not that he knew for sure, when he was trying so hard not to look at her every five minutes.

Quinn had more respect for the woman he was on a date with—normally. And it wasn't Lorie's fault his head was so messed up—oh, no, he *knew* whose fault it was. And right that minute she was using a thumb to brush something off Mitch's chin while she laughed.

'You want coffee?' Quinn willed Lorie to say no.

'I'd love some.'

Clare laughed at Mitch's antics as he rolled his eyes and made exaggerated noises of pleasure. He really was a nice guy, but it was like being on a date with a sibling, and instinctively Clare knew they both felt that way. It was just one of those things—no chemistry. Mutual liking, yes, but no spark. They could be friends, though, she felt.

'Okay, your turn.' Mitch loaded a fork with some of his chanterelle-filled corn crêpes.

It had seemed like a nice thing to do when neither of them could decide what to have from the menu, but Clare suddenly felt a little self-conscious about leaning across the table to share. Especially if by some miracle Quinn happened to look her way. Not that he'd done anything but devote his attention to Lorie all flipping night long, but even so…

As a compromise, she reached out her hand and took the fork, rolling her eyes the same way Mitch had. 'Mmm.'

'Amazing, isn't it?'

*'Mmm.'* She nodded, handing him back his fork.

When she sent the seeking tip of her tongue out to catch any lingering hint of the flavours from her lips she looked across the room again—and her gaze clashed with Quinn's.

He didn't even flinch.

He remained unmoved while holding her gaze in silent siege across the room. *She* wasn't unmoved. She could feel her pulse beating a salsa, could feel heat curling in her abdomen, her breathing was laboured. But Quinn just stared.

He didn't even blink.

'Clare?' Concern sounded in Mitch's voice.

When it took another moment for her to break eye contact, Mitch turned and looked over his shoulder. Quinn at least did him the courtesy of nodding in his direction, which was more than he'd managed for Clare.

Mitch then studied her face, and the knowing look that appeared in his eyes made Clare want to crawl under the table. He smiled softly. 'Do you want to leave?'

She was officially the worst date in the world. How was she supposed to look people in the face and give them dating advice when she was so bad at it herself? Do as I say…*not as I do…*

'No.' She smiled back at him, equally as softly.

'It's awkward for you with the boss here.'

Clare wished it was that simple. But Quinn being her boss had nothing to do with it. So she took a deep breath and laid her hand on Mitch's, squeezing as she spoke. 'It's fine—honestly. And I'm having fun. Why wouldn't I? You're a great guy.'

'That's almost as bad as being told I'm *nice*.'

She laughed, sliding her hand back across the table. 'You're more than nice. Because you're going to swap desserts with me too, aren't you? And that's the mark of a *great* guy—trust me.'

Why, oh, why couldn't she be attracted to a great guy for once in her life, instead of the kind of man who would inevitably break her heart? Was it so much to ask?

Quinn's impatience grew after the silent stand-off with Clare. He wanted to be as far away from her as humanly possible, especially after she'd looked at him that way, leaving him with a dull ache in his chest and a heavy knot of anger in his stomach.

The distance between them suddenly felt like a gap the size of the Grand Canyon. He hated that. Perversely, he wanted to be the one sitting there while she smiled the soft smile she used to use to haul him out of a dark mood—the very smile she'd just given Mitch before setting her hand on his. He wanted to be able to laugh with her the way they used to. He wanted the familiarity of the back-and-forth teasing that had brightened his days since he'd got to know her better.

He missed her. It didn't make any sense to him, not when he saw her every day. But he missed her.

The next morning he threw on a faded Giants' T-shirt and sweats before allowing the sights to blur together around him as he ran his usual route round Brooklyn

Heights and along the promenade. He did his best thinking while running. Things became clearer.

Usually.

He stopped at the end of the promenade and grabbed hold of the railing, bending over as he evened out his breathing and frowned at the Statue of Liberty across the shimmering bay, his heart still pounding in his chest.

Nope, catching his breath didn't help either.

So he pushed upright, turning and running harder towards home until the aching in his lungs distracted him again. But when he got to his front door and looked up he frowned harder; nowhere to run, nowhere to hide…

Clare was sitting on his stoop.

When she lifted her chin and casually looked him over, Quinn's body responded. She really had no idea what she did to him.

It took considerable effort to force nonchalance into his voice. 'You're up early.'

'Always been a morning person.' She lifted a thin newspaper off the step beside her and waved it at him. 'I kept the sports section for you. And I brought you some of that juice you like.'

Quinn's eyes narrowed as he braved a step closer, taking the sports section from her before he sat one step down and accepted the proffered juice.

'Is it my birthday already?'

Clare shrugged and leaned back against the brownstone wall that lined the steps. 'If you don't want it, don't drink it.'

After drinking half of it, Quinn set it down and then shook the paper open before laying it out on his knees. If she had something she wanted to say he reckoned she'd get to it soon enough.

'So how was the date with Lorie?'

He feigned interest in the paper. 'There won't be a second one, if that's what you're asking.'

'Why?'

'She ate food off my plate.' He shrugged. 'It makes me crazy when someone does that.'

Exasperation sounded in her voice. '*That's* the reason you're dismissing her after *one date*?'

'Up till then she'd been doing fine.'

'Well, she obviously wasn't that distasteful to you—your car wasn't here when I got home last night.'

Quinn took a silent breath to keep his impatience in check. 'At what time?'

When she hesitated, he held the breath he'd taken—inwardly cursing himself for giving her a hint of how curious he was about *her* date.

Fortunately for him, she didn't seem to notice. 'Just before midnight.'

'Mitch turned into a pumpkin, did he?'

'Very funny. I thought I talked to you about sleeping with someone on the first date.'

The edge to her voice brought his chin up, his gaze searching her eyes until she turned her face away. 'You let me skip the dating etiquette talk, remember?'

Quinn studied her for a long moment, the instinctive need to reassure her surprising him. He lowered his voice. 'I didn't sleep with her, O'Connor.'

'You just talked all night, did you?'

'No-o…I dropped her home and went to the club for a while. This whole jumping to conclusions thing working out for you, is it?' He let a half-smile loose.

'Well, it's not like your track record helps any.'

'There you go with that low opinion of me again.

If you'd bothered having that etiquette talk with me you might've discovered I'm not completely lacking in morals.'

While she mulled that one over he turned his attention back to the paper, calmly turning the page to make it look as if he was actually reading it.

'Well, maybe we should have that talk. That's four for four now, so something's not right.'

'I should string them along some, should I?'

'I'm not suggesting that—'

'Good—cos I think you'll find I do the opposite of that in general.' He raised a brow as he turned the page again. 'So how was *your* date?'

'It was…' she hesitated again '…nice.'

Quinn grimaced. 'Ouch—poor guy—what'd he do to deserve that? I thought you liked Mitch.'

'I do like him. He's—'

'Nice?' He lifted his chin again and saw the colour rising on her cheeks. That was the thing with creamy clear skin like Clare's—the slightest rise in colour was a dead giveaway. 'Nice enough for a second date?'

Clare hesitated for a third time, and when he dropped his gaze he saw her worrying her lower lip, the sight forming an unwarranted wave of warmth in his chest.

She exhaled. 'Probably not.'

Quinn nodded, guessing that looking pleased wouldn't endear him to her. 'Best not to string him along, then…'

It took a second, but Clare sighed deeply. 'Fine, you've made your point. But at least I didn't dismiss him offhand over something trivial. He didn't do anything wrong—it was me.'

Quinn's interest was piqued all the more. 'What did *you* do wrong?'

She avoided his gaze again, the thinning of her lips letting him know what it was costing her to tell him. 'I'm just out of practice, I guess; I couldn't relax.'

It hadn't looked that way to Quinn—but telling her that would be admitting he'd been watching. So that option was out. Option two might be to tell her she should try again, but he didn't want her to try again. Not if there was even the vaguest chance she might do it under his nose a second time.

He thought of something. 'Have you ever filled one of those questionnaires in?'

'No, of course I haven't—'

The idea began to grow. 'Maybe you should. You might be surprised what you learn about yourself. And it might give you a better idea what to look for in the next guy, don't you think?'

Clare's mouth opened.

But Quinn kept going. 'Yankees or Mets?'

'What?'

'Are you a Yankees or Mets fan? Can't have a divided house when it comes to sports—what if the guy you fall for takes his sports seriously and you're on the wrong side?' He tutted at her. 'I did say a different questionnaire for men and women might be a better idea.'

'I hate to be the one to tell you, but sports isn't high on the list of things that make a relationship work.' She looked highly indignant that he might think it was. 'A glorified game of rounders is hardly that big a deal in the greater scheme of things.'

Quinn shot her a look of outrage. 'I'll have you know that's my country's national sport you're talking about there, babe. A little respect please.'

'Don't call me babe.' She lifted a hand and began counting off her fingers. 'Kids, careers, goals for the future, similar backgrounds, shared hobbies…'

When she ran out of digits she frowned down at her hand and lifted the other one to repeat the process. Quinn cleared his throat and interrupted her.

'All more important than sports—I agree.' He let a lazy smile loose on her when she looked up at him. 'Little things can matter too, though. They count.'

'I'm not saying they don't. I just—'

'Like, for instance, I know if anyone dares set a cup of something hot down without a coaster it makes you crazy.'

'It leaves a ring.'

'Yeah.' He found his gaze drawn to a wisp of her hair caught in the breeze that had picked up. 'You told me. And I know no amount of expensive flowers will ever be as big a deal to you as a bunch of daisies…'

Clare's voice lowered, her mouth sliding into a soft smile that drew his attention to her lips as she formed the words. 'They're smiley flowers.'

Quinn looked up into her eyes, his voice lower too. 'Must be. Always make *you* smile, don't they?'

She nodded, smiling. So he kept going.

'Horror movies give you nightmares. Girl movies that make you cry actually make you happy.' Which had been a source of great amusement to him for a long while, but she knew that. 'So even though a guy might not get what the deal is with that, he should keep it in mind on movie night. Knowing the little things matters…'

She took a somewhat shaky breath. 'I guess so.'

'As does knowing the little things that'll bug

someone—like a person who eats off your plate or talks too much, or would rather spend a day in a spa than go play touch football in the park with the rest of your friends.' Something *they'd* done together dozens of times. and she knew he'd never brought another woman to. 'You should fill in one of your own questionnaires, O'Connor.'

Clare looked defeated. 'Maybe we should just forget the whole thing. It's obviously not working.'

To his amazement Quinn disagreed. 'You're not quitting on me that easy. If you even think about it that blind forfeit is gonna be a doozy. Trust me.'

Suddenly a third option came to him…

When they'd spent time together before he hadn't been so aware of her, had he? Maybe what they needed was a little more familiarity rather than the cavernous gap between them. It was worth a try…

He set the paper to one side and folded his arms across his chest. 'What you need is a no-pressure date. And we could combine it with the dating etiquette talk before you set me up again—two birds, one stone kinda thing.'

Clare's eye's widened. 'I'm not going on a date with *you*, if that's what you're suggesting.'

'A *practice* date with me.'

'*Any* kind of a date with you.'

Clare could feel her palms going clammy with nervous anticipation. He couldn't be serious.

Quinn merely blinked at her. 'It would be a good chance for us to try and get past all this awkwardness since the night at the club too, don't you think? Friends can go out for a night.' He nodded in agreement with himself. 'And we already agreed back at the start that

I'm a special case matchmaking-wise. You gotta admit I'm being pretty magnanimous about giving you a chance of winning.'

'Yes and why exactly *is* that?' It made her suspicious that there was something she didn't know. 'You find a way to cheat on these things ninety percent of the time…'

'I don't cheat. I think outside the box. You should take a trip out here some time—you might be surprised how much you like it.'

Which was a third generation Irish-American way of telling her she was boring and predictable, wasn't it?

'Last time I took a trip outside the box it didn't turn out so great for me.' She smirked.

'Too chicken to try again?'

Clare swallowed hard as he studied her with one of the intense stares that had been making her so uneasy of late. Thing was, now she knew *why* they made her so uneasy she really couldn't take a chance on *him* finding out. How could she ever face him again if he knew?

'Quinn…' She closed her eyes in agony when his name came out with a tortured edge that hinted at her discomfort. He really had no idea what he did to her.

When she opened her eyes he was still studying her. Heat immediately built inside her and radiated out over every pore of her body until she could feel the flush deepening on her cheeks. He could turn her inside out when he looked at her that way.

The devil's own smile appeared, and his voice was temptation itself. 'I promise you'll enjoy whatever we do.'

A worrying thought on a whole new level.

He nodded again. 'Monday night's good for me.'

Clare sighed. 'It's this kind of railroad tactic that'll lose you the right girl somewhere along the way, you know.'

'I'd heard a rumour it was about taking the bad with the good. And when I put my mind to it I can be *incredibly good.*' He gathered up the paper and the juice. 'I'll take that as a yes, then.'

When he pushed to his feet and stepped over her, the smile on his face was so smug Clare dearly wanted to hit him.

But she could survive *one date.*

She *could.*

She was pretty sure she could…

## CHAPTER SEVEN

'SO IS THIS ONE OF your usual date destinations?' Clare watched him lay out the contents of the large paper bags he'd made up at a deli on their way there.

'That's the conversation opener you'd go with on a real date.' Quinn shook his head. 'If we'd just met you wouldn't know I'd left a half million women sobbing all over Manhattan, would you?'

The simple answer to her question would have been no. He'd never brought a woman to the Monday night movie in Bryant Park. None of the women he'd dated would have appreciated it, whereas Clare's face had lit up the minute she'd known where they were going. And, yes, it could have been because it took some of the pressure off. But he knew Clare. Her enthusiasm had just as much to do with her love of the simple things in life. Quinn liked that about her, always had.

He also liked that she hadn't been to Manhattan's version of an open-air mass movie night before. It made paying someone to snag a space for them before the crowds descended worthwhile.

Clare curled her legs underneath her on the blanket, one fine-boned hand smoothing the pale green skirt of her summer dress before she folded her hands together in her lap. It was a dress he hadn't seen before, and Quinn liked that she might have bought it for their date. Elegantly simple, it flowed in around her legs to hint at their shape when she moved, subtle and sexy at the same time—Clare O'Connor in a nutshell.

When he'd seen her wearing it, it had made him think about the first time Jamie had brought her to meet everyone—when Quinn had wondered why someone as classy as her had fallen for Jamie. Jamie was a player—always had been, always would be. It hadn't affected his friendship with Quinn, though, even when they'd been rivals for the girls in high school. Not until Clare.

'What's the movie?'

'*Casablanca.*' He continued laying out the picnic, watching from the corner of his eye as she plucked a whispering strand of rich auburn hair from her cheek.

Amusement danced in her luminous eyes when she looked at him. 'Oh, you really pull out all the stops, don't you?'

'Unfortunately I don't have that much pull with the people who organize this. I should take the credit on a real date, though, shouldn't I?'

The recriminating frown was small and brief. 'Only if you make it clear you're not telling the truth.'

'Complete honesty from the start, huh?' He smiled. '*Man*, you're a tough date already.'

Smiling softly in return, she turned to observe the crowd, giving him a chance to study her profile.

'If you're honest from the get go there's less chance of trouble further down the line.'

Quinn knew her statement was a personal conviction. Having been sucked in by a pack of lies from Jamie, she wouldn't want to make the same mistake again. Trouble was, there were secrets he was keeping about what had happened with Jamie that landed Quinn squarely in the territory of trouble further down the line if she ever found out.

When her gaze swung back towards him he made himself smile. 'So when she asks if she looks fat in something…?'

A burst of musical laughter trickled through the air, and the lilt to her accent was more pronounced. 'Ah, now, that'd be different, that would.'

'Mmm. Thought it might…'

She shook her head. 'So, is this the kind of date you prefer? Not a fancy restaurant like Friday night?'

Digging out the bottle of sparkling water she'd chosen instead of wine, he shrugged his shoulders. 'Thought you'd enjoy this.'

He could still feel her gaze on him while he focused on filling plastic glasses. It was getting to the stage where he was completely aware of what she was doing at any given time, even without looking. And when he *was* looking it was becoming an obsession. If she brushed her hair back he would swear it sent a whisper of her scent towards him. If she breathed deep or sighed he could almost feel the air shift. And if she touched her hand to her face or her neck—or idly ran the tips of her fingers over her forearm while thinking—he would find himself mesmerized, wondering what it would feel like to touch her.

She was rapidly becoming addictive.

The thought made him frown, which Clare took as a need for reassurance. Her voice took on a soothingly soft tone that caressed his ears. 'I will. I've wanted to do this since I moved here…'

'Passed dating test number one, then, did I?'

'You did.'

When he looked up she turned away again, and Quinn felt the reappearance of the gap between them. He hated that gap—hated that its presence made him feel the need to reach out for her.

Instead he made an attempt at humour. 'And I haven't even got started yet…'

It didn't go down the way he'd hoped it would. Because instead of a smile he saw her throat convulse, her fingers clenching and releasing in her lap. 'You shouldn't try too hard on a first date; just be yourself and you'll do fine.'

She was handing him *advice* now?

'Thanks. I wouldn't have known that if you hadn't told me.' Quinn's tone was purposefully dry. It would be nice if she could place him somewhere between Casanova and a guy on his first prom date. She couldn't have it both ways.

She let the comment slide. 'So what do you normally do on a first date?'

'Depends…'

'On what?' Her gaze tangled with his again.

Quinn handed her a half-glass of chilled water, the accidental brushing of their fingers sending a jolt of awareness to his gut. 'On whether or not I'm trying to impress the woman I'm with.'

Long lashes flickered upwards. 'And you felt the need to impress *me*?'

He cocked a brow. 'After you stomped all over my male pride by suggesting I didn't know how to treat a woman on a date?'

'I didn't say that.'

'My ego heard it that way.'

Clare scowled. 'So in order to impress me you thought picnic and a movie, an apple pie kind of date. Whereas if I was one of your usual women I'd get the champagne and caviar date: expensive dinner, best seats at a sold out Broadway show, limo to drop me at my door. That's what you're saying?'

Not as it happened.

'Is that what you'd have preferred?' He managed to keep the frown off his face, but it took considerable effort. She made it sound as if he saw her as less somehow. When in actuality he'd spent more time thinking about where he'd take Clare than he'd ever thought about a date venue.

'Do you have some kind of sliding scale?'

'No, I don't have a sliding scale. And I think you should stop this line of questioning before we have an argument on our first date, don't you?'

'It's a *practice* date.'

'Then play the game. Make small talk like we've never met before.' Striving for patience, he stretched his legs out in front of him, leaned back, turned onto his side and then propped an elbow to rest his head on his palm. 'Tell me about Clare O'Connor…'

'You already know me inside out.'

No, she was becoming more of a mystery to him every day. How her mind worked, for instance. He hadn't a clue about *that*, and it might help if he did. 'Play nice, O'Connor. This is s'posed to be a practice run for you too, remember? Try entering into the spirit of things.'

Confusion flickered over the green of her eyes; there was a split second of indecision. Then her chin tilted to one side and a hint of a smile quirked the edges of her full mouth. The latter made Quinn suspicious—because unless he was very much mistaken the accompanying sparkling he could see in her eyes was *mischief.* What was she thinking *now*?

'Okay, then.' Setting her water down on the rug between them, she unfolded her legs, stretched them out in front of her as she turned onto her side. Then she casually propped one elbow so she could rest her head on her hand, a curtain of softly waving hair immediately covering it as she smiled a slow, mesmerizing smile.

'Hello, you…'

Quinn forgot to breathe. She was playing up to him. She was flirting with him as if they were on a real date.

Clare was smiling impishly. 'This is where you say hello to me. You could smile too—that would help.'

Okay. He'd play. His answering smile was deliberately slow. 'Hello, you.'

She chuckled throatily, the sound intensely sexual. 'Tell me about you and then I'll tell you about me.'

'I asked first.'

'Whatever happened to ladies first?'

'I'm *letting* the lady go first.' Quinn's smile grew—he couldn't have stopped it even if he'd wanted to. 'Tell me something I don't already know.'

Shaking her head against her hand, she sighed dramatically, rolling her eyes. And then, while raising her knees to get more comfortable on the blanket, she confessed, 'I can stick out my tongue and touch the end of my nose.'

A burst of deep laughter rumbled up out of his chest. 'No, you can't.'

'Oh, yes, I can.'

He jerked his chin at her. 'Go on, then.'

Rolling her narrow shoulders to limber up, she wiggled her nose, eyes shining when he laughed at her antics. And then she took a deep breath and calmly stuck her tongue out at him.

Lifting her free arm, she made a flourishing move of her hand, lifted her brows—and touched her forefinger to the end of her nose…

Making him laugh even more. 'You're a funny girl.'

She rewarded him with a full, engaging smile that lit up her face. 'Your turn.'

'I like to save my best moves for the end of the night.' He threw an exaggerated wink her way.

'And you're a funny guy.'

'My PA tells me that every day.'

'She must be a very patient woman.'

'Practically saint-like…' He nodded.

Clare made a sound that sounded distinctly like a snort. 'With a halo, no doubt.'

'Oh, I'd say she has her fair share of mischief tucked away somewhere. It just doesn't come out to play very often.' As it was now, for instance. And Quinn liked it. He liked it a whole lot. 'She should let her hair down every now and again.'

'You don't think she does?'

'No.' He shook his head, his gaze fixed steadily on hers as he purposefully lowered his voice. 'I think she's cautious about letting loose.'

'Do you, indeed?'

When he made an exaggerated nod she surprised him again. This time by leaning closer, her face a scant foot from his when she looked at him from beneath heavy lashes. 'Didn't anyone ever tell you you should never judge a book by its cover?'

And when she bit down on her lower lip to control her smile it was suddenly as plain as day to Quinn why Jamie had been so taken with her that he'd persuaded her to follow him across an ocean. He still didn't know why she'd followed. But what he *did know* was that now he'd got a glimpse of a different side of Clare he wanted more.

'And now I'm intrigued.'

When she lifted her head a little, and her hair fell into her eyes, he instinctively lifted a hand and brushed it back so he could see her, his fingertips lingering against her soft cheek for a brief second.

Clare's eyes widened in response, studying him with an open curiosity he'd never seen before. But instead of asking her about it, he smiled, letting his heavy hand drop as he pushed for more information.

'Were you a mischief-maker back in Ireland?'

It brought the impish smile back, her chin dropping as her hand rose to check he'd tucked the strand of hair away properly. 'I had my moments. Doesn't everyone in their teens?'

'What was it like growing up there?'

Clare searched his eyes, and then shifted her gaze to look at the people over his head. But he knew she wasn't seeing them. The wistfulness on her face told him she was across the Atlantic again, in the land his own ancestors had travelled from.

'I was happy—free—but kids who grow up on a farm have a lot of freedom. We ran riot in all weather, made secret huts, tried to catch wild rabbits so we could keep them as pets, searched for fairies in the woods...'

Quinn was spellbound. By her expression as she shared the memories as much as by the picture she'd painted. Why had he never noticed how beautiful she was? Had he ever looked at her properly? He'd always thought she was pretty, but now…

'Find any?'

'Rabbits or fairies?'

'Fairies.'

'Nah.' She gave him a sideways, twinkle-eyed glance, lowering her voice as if sharing a secret. 'They're slippery wee things are fairies.'

'I'd heard that…'

The fact he'd lowered his voice to a similar level seemed to make her eyelids heavy. 'We had a fairy ring in the woods. So when we were little we were convinced they couldn't be that far away. My mother encouraged us to search for them—I think it gave her peace for a few hours. Three kids under the age of ten can be tiring.'

'I know.' It had been the same with the four in the Cassidy household when Quinn had been growing up. 'You should try it with a house full of boys.'

Her lashes lowered, making Quinn feel the need to crook a finger under her chin so he could continue looking into her eyes. 'I'd love a house full of boys. They'd love me their whole lives. Whereas a girl will have to hate me for at least half her teenage years; it's traditional she'll think I'm ruining her life…'

Long lashes rose, oh, so slowly. And Quinn smiled. He'd never thought of Clare with kids and he had no idea why. She'd be a great mom some day. She'd make sure they were ten minutes early for every school activity, she'd paint pictures of daisies with little girls—

make sure boys knew all the right things to say to any girl they were thinking of dating…

'So you don't think pets can be a substitute for a family, then, I take it?'

She caught the reference and scowled playfully at him, dragging another chuckle of laughter free from deep inside his chest.

Which made her laugh softly in return. 'No, I don't. Pets *and* a family, that's the box I'd tick. Every kid should have a dog.'

Quinn's smile faltered. Had she got that off his questionnaire? He racked his brain to see if he could remember finding the question when he'd looked for it.

Clare shifted suddenly, pushing upwards and curling her legs back underneath her as she reached for some of the cheeses he'd set out. 'What were you like as a kid?'

A date with Clare was like riding a rollercoaster. Quinn shook his head as he pushed up into a similar position to hers, because his childhood couldn't have been more different from hers if it had tried.

'You want crackers with that?'

Oh, he was a clever one, wasn't he? Clare took a much needed inward breath as she realised what had just happened. He'd done exactly what match number three had said he'd done with her—steered the conversation onto her, so that she'd end up doing all the talking. Well, he needn't think he was getting away with it. A practice date he wanted; a practice date he'd get. And she might be a tad rusty but she was pretty sure it involved a two-way conversation…

Then she remembered something. 'You had a nickname, didn't you? I remember Evan and Morgan keeping you going about it. What was it again?'

A quick glance in his direction saw his wide chest rise and fall before his gravelly voice grumbled back the answer. 'Scrapper.'

Lifting her chin so she could look into his amazing eyes, she smiled to encourage him to keep going. 'How'd you get landed with that, then?'

Quinn cocked a brow at her.

She smiled all the more. 'Got into a few fights, did we?'

'More than a few.'

'How come?'

'Anger management issues.'

Watching while he loaded a cracker with cheese, Clare felt a dull ache forming in her chest. 'What were you angry about?'

'I was nine when I got that nickname. You don't know why you're angry back then; you just know you are.'

He'd been getting into regular fights at nine? How bad had they been? Why hadn't anyone done anything to stop it happening? Had he been bullied? The Quinn she knew was the most in control man she'd ever met. He could defuse a difficult situation with a single glare. Had he learned that at some point because he'd *had to*?

The ache became a bubble of emotion. 'But you know now, don't you?'

'Yup.' He popped an entire heavily laden cracker into his mouth, his gaze straying out over the crowd.

Another memory came to her: she'd tried talking to Quinn about his past before, hadn't she? Way back at the start, when Jamie had first introduced her to his friends. She'd tried making conversation on the usual subjects, family, work, the weather… And Quinn had been so unresponsive she'd simply assumed he didn't like her much, so she'd stopped trying. But add that to the recent information from his date with match number three and she suddenly had a different picture. So she waited.

Opening up wasn't something that came easily to him. She got that now.

Eventually Quinn looked at her from the corner of his eye as he slapped large palms on jean-clad hips to remove residual crumbs. When she continued waiting in silence, he shook his head and grumbled out another piece of the puzzle. 'I met Morgan, Jamie and Evan the day I got that nickname…'

The slant of wickedly sensual lips formed a thin line before he continued, his voice lacking in emotion. Not even a hint of sentiment at the memory of the first time he'd met the men who'd been his best friends ever since—well—two of them anyway…

'It was my first day at school after we moved to Brooklyn from Queens. Word had got around about my old man before I got there—parents gossiping, probably. And when some of the boys made comments I didn't take kindly to—I took them on.' He shrugged. 'The guys broke it up and walked me home. I was pretty banged up.'

Clare's brows wavered in question. 'How many did you take on?'

'Five.'

*On his own?* The odds alone told her what state of *banged up* he must have been in. She thought of a nine-year-old Quinn, all bloody and bruised, being walked home by his new protectors—more than likely determined not to shed a single tear in front of them—and it broke her heart. She knew his father had died. How could those kids have said dreadful things to him when he'd just lost his father?

The anguish she felt must have shown in her eyes, because the smile he gave her was dangerous—doubly so when it was Quinn wearing it. It was a side to him she'd never seen up close before.

'Don't worry—I learned my lesson that day, picked up a move or two after that. And a decade of scrapping made me one heck of a bouncer at the first club I worked.'

Despite his reaction to what he obviously considered pity, Clare couldn't help it. Her jaw dropped. *That* was where he'd started his career with clubs—breaking up fights? New York was the best city in the world, but for a while it had been rough in places. He could have been seriously hurt—and if anything had happened…

She might never have met him.

Quinn misinterpreted her reaction again. 'Guess I should skip this little talk on the first date? Knew there was a reason I hadn't done it before.'

'Did you get in any trouble?'

'No—but thanks for the vote of confidence. First time I dealt with a cop was the night I got offered the security gig.'

*Again* he'd misinterpreted her. Clare was frowning in annoyance as much as confusion, because he did that *a lot.* And he should know her better. 'That wasn't what I meant. A police officer offered you the job?'

'Me and the guys were heading home when a fight got started. Some guy hit a woman—so I put him down and kept him there till the cops arrived. That's when the club offered me the job.' He jerked his shoulders again.

'Apparently I did it faster and with less fuss than anyone they'd ever seen before. Practice makes perfect, they say. And I'd got to the point in my life where I believed the best offence was a good defence.'

Clare stared at him, which started the beginnings of another dark frown on his face. 'So I wasn't your first damsel in distress, then?'

The frown dissipated. 'Guess not.'

When he searched her eyes for the longest time, Clare's heart thudded hard against her breastbone—a thought making her breath catch. Had he thought telling her about his past would change how she saw him? Didn't he know the fact he'd not only stayed out of trouble but turned himself into a respected self-made millionaire before thirty only made her respect him *more*? He was living, breathing proof of the American dream.

She thought he was amazing.

Unable to hold his intense gaze any longer, she dropped her chin and played at putting cheese on a cracker—being particularly fussy about the angles until she got her emotions under control.

'That's why you ended up owning clubs in the end?'

'I own clubs because they make money.'

'And money is all that matters?'

'Matters when you don't have it.'

Her gaze rose again to find him studying her, then he took a breath and turned to study the large screen where the movie would play.

'There are worse ways of making money.' He smiled, glancing at her from the corner of his eye. 'Opening night for the Manhattan one was fun, though, wasn't it?'

Clare smiled at the shared memory. 'It was.'

As manically insane as it had been on the run-up, she knew it had been the kind of night she'd never forget. When Quinn had offered her a job he'd still been at the planning stages. But one by one and side by side they'd worked their way through the many lists Clare had made to keep everything on schedule until they had had the kind of opening that had been the talk of New York and beyond for weeks afterwards.

It had been the first time she'd really felt her decision to stay in New York had been the right one. She had felt she'd achieved something—helped build something—and in a small way she'd felt as if she'd repaid a few of the many favours she owed Quinn. Best of all, they'd become friends along the way…

Or she'd thought they had.

'How did you afford the first one?'

And just like that he was frowning again. She'd never known his moods to fluctuate as much as they had of late.

'What difference does it make?'

Clare kept her voice purposefully soft. 'None. I'd just like to know.'

'All that matters is the first one made enough for the second one and the second made triple what the first one did…Thanks to Morgan's investment advice and the thousands of dollars VIP members pay annually I don't lose any sleep when bills come in.'

He took another breath and looked over the crowd.

Except now Clare wanted to know even more than she had before. He had a lesson or two to learn about reverse psychology. 'I've just figured out why it is I don't know you as well as I thought I did.'

When he didn't say anything in reply she smiled at his profile. 'Don't you want to know what I figured?'

'I'm sure you'll tell me regardless.'

'I will.' She waited until he glanced at her again. 'It's because you don't want me to.'

Quinn looked confused by the reasoning. 'That's not true.'

'Isn't it?'

'Who I was back then isn't who I am now.'

'But it's *a part* of who you are now…'

'You're like a dog with a bone, you know that?' He shook his head, turning so he could study her eyes with open curiosity. 'You know me well enough, O'Connor—little bit more than most, as it happens. Even before that questionnaire of yours. Why does it suddenly matter now?'

That was the million-dollar question, really. But Clare simply studied him right on back. And when she smiled softly at him it took a moment, but soon enough the light reappeared in his eyes and his mouth slid into an answering smile. Making her smile all the more…

'Okay, then, how did you learn the least-fuss method for your good defence?'

He chuckled ruefully, letting her know she wasn't fooling him with her change of subject. 'I lived in the local boxing club—fought in the ring as a junior to deal with the anger management.'

'Really?'

'Really. Even broke my nose, *twice*.'

'There's nothing wrong with your nose.' She studied it just to be sure.

'Second time straightened it some.'

When she looked back into his eyes she saw the light twinkling, and her jaw dropped with a gasp of mock outrage.

*'Fibber.'*

Deep, rumbling laughter echoed up from his chest and Clare felt her heart expand. See, now, there he was. *That* was the Quinn she knew. She'd missed him so very much.

'Had you for a minute…'

'Did not.'

'Did so.'

She lifted a handful of crackers and flung them at his chest, laughing with him when he rocked backwards, scrambling to catch them only to have them disintegrate in his large hands, scattering crumbs everywhere.

'You're a dreadful date, Quinn Cassidy.'

'No, I'm not.' His vivid eyes danced with silent laughter. 'And the first date is a trial run. By date three I'd win you over.'

It was a theory he could have done with putting into practice on some of the dates she'd sent him on. Before she could point out there wouldn't be a second date, never mind a third, with her, the huge screen came to life and Clare exhaled.

*Saved by Humphrey Bogart.*

Probably just as well. Because the fact there wouldn't be other dates with him left Clare's heart heavy. And that really didn't bode well…

# CHAPTER EIGHT

IT STARTED TO RAIN the second the credits rolled. But when Quinn raised a hand to hail a cab, Clare tugged on his sleeve.

'Can we take the subway? The novelty hasn't worn off for me yet.'

Quinn normally avoided the crowds and the stifling heat at all costs, especially in summer. But her enthusiasm for the simplest of things was infectious, so he gave in. They weren't the only ones with the same idea; people crowded down the stone steps to stand in the ridiculous heat of the platform at Forty-Second Street.

The wave of bodies moved forward *en masse* when the train arrived, leaving Quinn and Clare standing in the packed compartment, which for the life of him Quinn couldn't find a reason to be unhappy about. Especially with Clare close enough for him to catch the scent of springtime from her hair. So instead he leaned down and teased her with a grumble of mock complaint.

'Oh, yeah, this was a great idea—very romantic end to the evening.'

Clare wrapped her fingers around a metal pole,

smiling over her shoulder at him as the doors slid shut. 'Just think of the good impression you're making on your carbon footprint.'

'It's not my carbon footprint I was trying to impress…'

'If you really were trying to impress me then you did fine with the movie and the picnic. It's the kind of night a girl doesn't forget too fast.'

An outdoor movie and a picnic in the park were the way to a girl's heart? Who knew? But Quinn knew he wouldn't forget it either. And he wouldn't be able to take another woman to Bryant Park without thinking of his night there with Clare.

The train jolted to a halt at the next stop, rocking Clare back on her heels. Quinn automatically lifted an arm and snaked it around her narrow waist to steady her—drawing her close. For a moment she tensed, the way she had the night he'd carried her, glancing sharply over her shoulder. Then he felt her take a deep breath and her slight body relaxed into his, curves moulding into dips and planes as if she'd been there hundreds of times and knew exactly where she would fit.

As was now usual, Quinn's body reacted. Meaning he had to focus on a random point down the compartment to give him something else to think about. So much for his familiarity theory…and his control theory… and…

The doors slid open, letting in more hot air. People got out; people got in. Then the doors slid shut again and the train jumped forwards.

Clare shifted her weight from one foot to the other, her body sliding against his as if she was dancing to some kind of silently sensual melody. It made Quinn close his eyes, frowning as the need to harness his physical reaction like an adult was overridden by a sudden vision of dancing with her. On the back of his eyelids he could see the play-by-play movie of it. He was turning her around in his arms, placing her hands on the back of his neck one by one, and then drawing her close, her breasts pressed tight against his chest, her hips swaying from side to side…

He snapped his eyes open. Now he was being tugged into erotic fantasies. By *Clare.*

Then he made the mistake of glancing down over her shoulder—in time to see a tiny trickle of moisture run from her collarbone down into the dark valley between her breasts. He stifled a groan.

Never had he felt so cornered by a woman: trapped deep underground in a dark tunnel in a compartment packed with people he barely noticed—and Clare pressed close enough to feel what she was doing to him.

She turned a little, her chin lifting and long lashes rising until her darkened green gaze was impossibly tangled with his. She even damped her lips with the tempting tip of her tongue.

Now Quinn's chest ached with the need for oxygen—the need to kiss her was so primal that his head was lowering before he had time to think about the consequences…

The train jerked to a halt again, bringing him back to his senses. So when a woman seated next to them stood up, Quinn practically manhandled Clare into the space. There. That was better. Now maybe he could breathe.

Clare being Clare, she spotted an elderly man behind him and immediately stood up to offer him her seat.

Even more frustratingly she returned to where she'd been before—this time facing him while holding the metal bar, her eyes sparkling with what looked like comprehension. She knew, didn't she? Knew what she was doing to him and wasn't the least bit upset about it. Well, if that was the case and she played up to him again, then all bets were off—new rules, new game.

Quinn's blood rushed faster at the thought of it.

She smiled. 'I think I can manage not to fall over this time…'

Meaning she was amused at his concern for her, or meaning she'd known he was about to kiss her and was letting him off the hook?

Quinn bent his knees and ducked his head to look out of the windows. 'Couple more stops.'

When he risked another look at her she lifted her finely arched brows. 'Are you okay? You look flushed.'

Quinn cleared his throat, purposely keeping the sound low so she wouldn't hear. 'I'd forgotten how hot it is down here.'

When he frowned at the double entendre she smiled all the more. 'It has all day to build up. But yeah, it's hot…'

Then she upped the ante by lifting a hand to the front of her dress and flapping the material against her breasts—which automatically drew his gaze downwards. It would serve her right if he reached out and hauled her in to kiss her until she was as affected as he was by their 'pretend date'. Quinn was hanging by a thread.

But she obviously wasn't as caught up in the moment as he was. When the train stopped again and *he* was the one that rocked towards *her* she giggled girlishly at his expression. Then she had the unmitigated gall to smile at another man as he walked past her to get to the doors.

*Right under Quinn's nose.*

So that was how she was playing it. She was on a pretend date with her best buddy after all. Part of the genius idea had been to help her ease back into the dating game. She'd tell him that if he called her on it too, wouldn't she?

It was just a shame the idea of her flirting even casually with someone else irritated him so thoroughly. That a part of him was now determined to make it very clear who it was she was with. So when the random guy smiled at her again as he stepped off the train, Quinn stepped closer, glaring at the man. Who in turn had the good sense to leave while Quinn lifted his hands to Clare's shoulders to turn her round, hauling her firmly against his body for the second time.

'What are you doing?' She looked down at his arms as they both circled her waist and held her tight. 'I can—'

'Shh.' He placed his cheek next to her silky soft hair and grumbled into her ear. 'If we were on a date this is exactly what I'd be doing about now. Play by the rules, O'Connor…'

*Play by the rules?* It was the second time he'd said that. Hadn't she played by the rules all night long? Hadn't she forgotten it was a pretend date entirely too much for her own good? Hadn't she—for a brief moment of insanity—been completely overwhelmed by the hope he was going to kiss her?

And, heaven help her, it was the most wonderful case of insanity she'd ever experienced. Just as crazy as it was to feel so right being held by him, with her body pressed so tight against his and his arms wrapped so firmly around her waist. Oh, Lord but it felt good.

Quinn was hard and lean, coiled muscle and heated skin and warm breath against her cheek. And he smelled sensational. Clare had never felt so very alive.

When his thumbs absentmindedly brushed back and forth against the base of her ribs she closed her eyes and leaned her head back against his shoulder, surrendering to sensation. She could have stayed there a lot longer—except the train was already slowing down…

Quinn immediately released her, stunning her when he tangled his long fingers with hers, her downward glance simply met with a gruff 'C'mon.'

It was still raining outside. And with a sideways glance and a smile that made her smile ridiculously back at him he asked, 'Can you run?'

Clare lifted her chin. 'Can you keep up with me?'

It was an empty challenge for someone who ran for miles round Brooklyn every day regardless of the weather. But with another smile and a squeeze of his fingers he glanced down at her low heels and back up into her eyes.

'I'll give it a shot.'

So they ran. The warm summer rain had soaked them through to the skin by the time they arrived breathless and laughing at the brownstone and Quinn saw her all the way to her door, still holding her hand while she fitted her key in the lock.

Heart pounding from exertion and a rising sense of anticipation, Clare looked down at their hands, watching as raindrops trickled off his skin onto hers.

'I need—' When her voice sounded thready, even to

her own ears, she took a second to control her voice. 'I kind of need that hand. It's attached to the rest of me.'

Lifting her lashes, she found his head bowed, wet fingers sliding over wet fingers while he watched. And then his chin rose, his eyes dark pools in the dim light, his face filled with shadows. But she didn't need better light to see him—he was Quinn—she could see him with her eyes closed.

As if the thought was a suggestion, Clare felt her eyelids growing heavy.

'For future reference, where does kissing on the doorstep fall in the dating etiquette rules?'

'Erm…' Clare nodded, her voice thready again '…I'd say that was under optional…or…'

In the shadows of his face she saw a smile forming, the sight making her heart flip-flop almost painfully.

'Or?'

If he didn't kiss her she might have to kill him. 'Or…at your own discretion…'

'Good to know.'

Clare held her breath. Quinn squeezed her fingers. Then he loosened them, sliding them free so slowly she felt the loss all the way to the pit of her soul. When he spoke his voice was so low she had to strain to hear over the sound of raindrops on concrete, on the leaves of the trees lining the street, bouncing off cars…

'Night, O'Connor…'

What? He was leaving? He wasn't going to kiss her?

Of course he wasn't going to kiss her; Clare felt like a complete idiot. They were *friends.* She was the cute girl who lived downstairs. He could have any woman he wanted in the whole of New York…

She'd never felt so foolish—even when Jamie had

left her to face all those guests alone. No, not alone. He'd left her with the best man. *The best man*; it was so ironic Clare almost laughed.

Quinn hadn't moved. And neither had Clare; her laboured breathing was nothing to do with the run they'd made and everything to do with how much she ached for a kiss she shouldn't want so desperately.

From somewhere she found the power of speech again. 'Night, Quinn.'

But he still didn't move. Didn't he know she was slowly dying in front of him?

The air caught in her lungs when his large hands rose and turned—knuckles brushing wet tendrils of hair off her cheeks in heartbreakingly gentle sweeps. The simple touch closed her heavy eyelids while the air left her lungs in one endless breath. How could a man with his experience not know what he was doing to her? The Quinn she knew would never torture her so severely.

'You should go inside.' The rough timbre of his voice was the sexiest thing she had ever heard.

'I should.'

But not before he left. She doubted she could get her feet to move. Every shuddering breath she took added to the yearning that had developed inside her, a shaking starting at her knees and gradually making its way upwards. The word *please* hovered precariously on the tip of her tongue…

If he didn't leave soon then she was going to make such a complete and utter twit of herself.

'I'll see you tomorrow.' Quinn's hands turned over, the very tips of his fingers whispering the last strands of hair off her cheeks.

Somehow Clare forced her eyes open, her ears hearing her voice say 'You will' while her heart yelled, *Don't go.*

After what felt like an eternity, he took a deep breath. 'Couldn't you just run your dumb matchmaking thing from my offices?'

Clare blinked up at him. Huh? Had she just missed something in the haze? Not that it wasn't the kind of suggestion she mightn't have considered before they'd made the stupid bet, but—

She shook her head to make her brain work. 'If you still think it's dumb then why are you doing it?'

Quinn's fingers stilled. 'If you're like this on a date then how come you're still hiding?'

'I'm not hiding. I just haven't met anyone I wanted to date…' It took all her strength not to add *until now* to the end of the sentence. Hadn't it occurred to him she'd been the way she had on their pretend date because she was with someone she already cared about? Maybe a little too much for what was supposedly a platonic relationship.

Quinn's arms dropped to his sides. 'Think about the office share—we could move things around some.'

'I can't keep relying on you to help me out.'

'Yeah, you can.'

No, she couldn't. Not any more. What had been tentative plans a few weeks ago were going to have to become more solid. She knew he'd always be there if she needed him—as a friend. And she loved that. She did. But she knew the relationship they had couldn't stay the same any more. Not if she was falling for him…

Quinn tilted his head back, letting the rain wash over his face as he stepped away from her. He dropped his chin as he spoke. 'Just think about it, O'Connor.'

Then he turned. When he took the steps two at a time and was on the pavement, a lucid thought finally entered Clare's head.

'Quinn?' She stepped forward.

He stopped, the street lights making it easier for her to see his face. 'Yes?'

'Are you doing all this matchmaking stuff to try and stop me from leaving work? Is that what this is all about?' A glimmer of hope sparked in her chest. If he wanted to keep her close by then maybe he cared as much as she did. Maybe he would miss her. Maybe, just maybe, that was a place to start?

Quinn frowned, glancing down the street and back before he replied, 'How honest do you want me to be about that?'

'Completely—as always.' She smiled somewhat tremulously, even though she knew she shouldn't. If he'd thought the whole bet up as part of some devious plan to keep her working for him then she should at least be miffed. It just wasn't easy to feel that way under the current circumstances. 'Any kind of lie breaks trust, remember? So are you?'

'You see everything in black and white, don't you? None of the hundreds of shades of grey in between…'

She shook her head, unable to understand how they'd got to where they were when not five minutes ago—

'Straight answer to a straight question—I just think if more people thought that way there'd be less heartache in the world.'

He looked down the street again.

Clare watched him push his hands into the pockets of his jeans. 'You could have told me you wanted me to stay.'

When he clenched his jaw, Clare willed him to talk to her. She'd never felt so far away from him. And it hurt. If he just said he wanted her to stay they could at least forget the dumb bet—because she really, really didn't want to matchmake for him any more.

'Go in, Clare.'

When he turned she took another step forward. 'Try it: "Clare, I want you to stay."'

With his profile turned to her she could see the clench of his jaw more clearly. 'That's all it would take, is it? You'd be content working for me and living here and never wanting more than that?'

Now, there was a question. She'd been happy working for him and living in the basement apartment. But never wanting more than that? *From him?* If that was even what he'd meant. It could simply have been a reference to the fact he thought she was hiding away and avoiding dating by using him as some kind of substitute boyfriend. If he'd meant the latter then her answer would certainly be less complicated. But if he'd meant the former—did she want more *from him*? Well, a little encouragement might help, a sign, a flicker of…*anything*…that might indicate *he* was interested in there being more…

Clare floundered in a sea of uncertainty.

And while she did Quinn walked away.

# CHAPTER NINE

'YOU DID *WHAT*?'

'It was a practice date.'

Madison laughed incredulously. 'The king of dating needed practice? I'm not buying it. Sorry.'

Clare tucked the receiver firmly between her shoulder and her ear. 'It wasn't my idea.'

'But you agreed to it.'

'Have you ever tried changing Quinn's mind when he sets it on something?' She practically growled at the file of a woman who was a ninety-four percent match for Quinn, immediately setting it on a teetering pile of discarded files. 'It made sense because he wasn't getting past the first date with any of his matches. I needed to find out why…'

'What *did* you find out?' Madison sounded highly amused. 'Tell all. Don't skip a single detail.'

'He didn't do anything wrong. That's just it. This whole thing is making me crazy.' She sighed again, feeling distinctly as if she was carrying the weight of the world on her shoulders. Hence the phone call for moral support. 'How do I get out of this dumb bet?'

'Oh, like hell you're getting out of it. You should hear

the debates we've been having with Morgan and Evan—you know they hero worship Quinn because of his rep with women? They think Quinn settling down is the end of an era. We think they're scared silly cos Quinn settling down means they might be next.' She paused for a moment. 'Do you think he's serious about it?'

'About settling down? I don't know. All I know is we've done nothing but bicker since it started.'

There was a much longer pause, then, *'Okay.'*

'What does *that* mean?'

'Let me ask you this—how long since you took a trip to Tiffany's for one of those little blue boxes?'

'Too long.' And she missed it. Spending hours browsing around the serene calm of the iconic store had been one of her favourite things to do. She should make a trip in her lunch break to see if it helped; it would be nice to find some sense of inner peace *somewhere.* Then it hit her.

'You think it's a sign he's got sick of playing the field, don't you?'

'That didn't occur to you?'

Obviously not. A small part of her had really believed he was playing some kind of game with her, hadn't it? There had certainly been clues along the way: the look in his eyes when he'd made the bet to begin with, his irreverence with the questionnaire, the ridiculous excuses for the lack of second dates—and that had been before she'd thought he'd only agreed to it as a way of getting her to stay put.

But if the lack of need for Tiffany's gifts was a sign he really was ready to settle down, then…

'Well…that'll be me moving out sooner rather than

later, won't it?' She'd mumbled under her breath but her friend heard every word.

'You're seriously thinking about moving out?' Madison's voice was filled with incredulity. 'When Morgan asked me about it I thought he was insane. Do you know how many people would give their right arm for an apartment like yours in Brooklyn Heights? That house of Quinn's has to be worth millions now.'

'*Morgan* asked you about me moving out?' Clare shook her head, frowning in confusion. 'When did that happen?'

'Not long after the bet was made. He even made me double check with Erin; wouldn't get off my case till I did. Apparently Quinn said something about—'

'*Quinn* did?' He'd been talking to Morgan about her moving out? What was he doing—looking for potential replacements before she'd even packed a bag? She hadn't said she was planning on going anywhere that soon! Did he want her to go? Was *that* it? Yes, she wanted to be able to afford her own place one day, and, yes, she would have to move if Quinn settled down with someone—what new wife would want a female friend of her husband's living downstairs from them? But Clare hadn't planned on going anywhere for a good while yet and she loved that apartment. Leaving it would be—

'Morgan seemed to think Quinn wasn't too pleased about you going, if that helps any.'

It did help—some.

Taking a deep breath and puffing her cheeks out as she exhaled, she leaned her elbows on her desk while she added the new information to the myriad of confusion she was already struggling with. There was really only one way to get out of the mess. What she should have done to begin with, and then she could have avoided *all* of the confusion. Things could have stayed the way they were. When she'd been *happy*...

The choice was clear. She wasn't going to matchmake for him any more. She was done. Even if it meant wearing a T-shirt that said 'Loser' as her forfeit. He could go out and find someone to make a commitment to on his own. And while he did she was going to work night and day to get the matchmaking up and running as a viable business. Then she could quit working for him sooner rather than later. And she could afford a place of her own too.

If he *had* made the bet as an underhanded way to get her to stay, then it had just backfired. Because he hadn't been asking if she wanted more *from him*, had he? Oh, no. If Quinn Cassidy was the remotest little bit interested in her that way he'd have done something about it. It wasn't as if he was famous for being the least little bit behind the door when it came to women...

Clare wasn't confused any more. She knew exactly where she stood. Lord, but she needed ice cream. 'I've gotta go—I have a gazillion things to do this afternoon before we go to Giovanni's.'

'Is Quinn going?'

'Course he's going. Why wouldn't he?' Things had been complicated beyond belief for Clare before the phone call with Madison, but Quinn didn't know that. So why wouldn't life go on the way it always had as far as he was concerned?

'Because it's the scene of the crime and all that...' Madison joked.

Clare smiled half-heartedly. 'Not helping. Just be a good girl and help me have fun later, okay?'

'It's that bad?'

'It's that bad.'

'Then it's a deal.'

'What's the deal with you and Clare?'

Quinn shot a frown at Morgan. 'Meaning?'

Morgan glanced at the two girls at the bottom of the table to make sure they were distracted enough not to overhear their low-toned conversation. He turned his back on them just to be sure. 'She's acting weird.'

'Weird how?'

Quinn did his best not to look at her. He'd barely been able to keep his eyes off her all night as it was, but that was what he got for being out of the office so much in the last forty-eight hours. Apparently he was so addicted to her he physically ached when she wasn't nearby. He wasn't the least bit happy about that.

Morgan shrugged. 'She's too bright—she laughs just a little too loud—like she's forcing herself to have a good time but she's not, if you know what I mean. Have you two had a fight?'

'No.' When he focused his attention on the thumb nail he was using to pick at the label on his bottle he could feel Morgan's frown.

'Something's going on, though.'

'Leave it be, Morgan.'

Quinn leaned back in his chair and gave in to his need for a fix of Clare—his mood quickly darkening when he spotted her chatting to some guy he'd never set eyes on before. The guy was laughing with her—and leaning close to listen to what she was saying—

When he set a hand on the small of her back Quinn was on his feet before Morgan had finished asking 'What's wrong?'

He saw her eyes widen in question as he worked his way through the tables. But he simply smiled back, stepping past the shorter guy to stand at her side and dismissing him with a quick glance before he placed an arm around her waist.

'You want dessert?'

Clare gaped at him. 'Excuse me?'

'We were just thinking about ordering dessert, so I thought I'd see if you wanted anything.' He shot her new friend a calm glare. 'This guy bugging you?'

Aiming an embarrassed smile at her new friend while removing Quinn's arm, Clare took hold of his hand and started moving away. 'I'm glad it went well for you, Sam. Good to see you.'

'You too, Clare. Thanks again.'

She nodded, tightening her fingers around Quinn's and tugging harder. 'Bye, Sam.'

Two steps away, she smiled through gritted teeth. 'Now we're going outside, where you can tell me just what you think you're doing.'

A quick check across the room was enough to confirm the suspicion that four pairs of eyes were watching them, so Quinn smiled for their benefit as he pushed open the door. 'You like dessert.'

'*I* like ice cream—*you* like dessert. Where do you get off coming on all Neanderthal man in front of one of my clients?'

*Another* client? How many clients did she have? They were everywhere. But it wasn't the fact that he'd just made a fool of himself so much as the fact she'd let go of his hand as if it had burnt her the second the door closed that made Quinn frown at her the way he did.

'Hasn't he ever heard of *office hours*?'

'Last time a client visited me during office hours *you* didn't like it.' She marched down the street, stopping on the kerbside where she swung round, her arms lifting and dropping. 'I've had it. I swear. You're making me crazy. I can't keep smiling and pretending everything's fine when it's not. Tonight has been the worst night I've ever had out with the gang. They've done nothing but watch us the whole time. I feel like we're some kind of *sideshow*!'

'They're just curious about how the bet is going.'

At least he hoped that was all it was. Frankly he didn't need any outside pressure or, heaven forbid—because the thought alone made him shudder—*advice.* 'It was made here—it's only natural they're thinking about it when we're at the scene of the crime.'

Clare's eyes narrowed. 'What did you just call it?'

The deathly calm edge to her voice made him frown again. 'Scene of the crime. Why?'

'That's what Madison called it on the phone today.'

'It's a common phrase.'

Her hands rose to the curve of her hips. 'Have you been talking to them about this? Because if this is some big joke and you've all been making with the funnies behind my back—'

Quinn's brows quirked. 'Yeah, cos I'm famous for being a big one for talking about my private life, aren't I? You're overreacting just a tad here, don't you think?'

Clare took a minute to debate it in her head before taking a breath that lifted her small breasts beneath her sleeveless blouse. Then she looked away from him, focusing on the people milling along the street in the humid evening air while she blinked hard and worried on her lower lip.

When she spoke her voice was thready. 'I don't want to do this any more. You win the bet.'

'Why?'

Quinn held his breath while he watched her struggling with an answer, her hands lifting from her hips so she could fold her arms defensively across her breasts. 'Because I don't want to matchmake for you.'

'Why?' His feet carried him a step closer to her.

When her gaze met his again he could see the lights from restaurants and passing cars sparkle in the glittering tears in her eyes. She was genuinely upset. Even though his very bones ached with the need to do something to fix it, he stood his ground, clenching his hands into fists so he wouldn't reach for her. He just needed her to say the words—and then he'd know crossing the line wouldn't be a big mistake…

Silently he willed her to say them.

Instead she shrugged her shoulders all the way up to her ears. 'I just want to go back to the way we were before all this started.'

It hadn't been all that long ago he'd told himself he wanted the same thing, but now… 'Clare—'

'So I think we should just drop all this and give each other a little space, don't you?'

Panic billowed up inside him, and the appearance of outward calm was costing him. 'I don't need space.'

Quinn's chest cramped at the anguish he could see in her eyes. It brought him another step closer before she added, 'Well, it's not like we've been the same since we made the bet, is it? Some space might do us good.' Her throat convulsed. 'I have plenty of holiday time chalked up. I might take a break. I'd make sure everything was up to date, obviously…or you could hire a temp…'

Now he was crowding her? He forced his feet not to take him any closer while she looked so fragile. How was he crowding her? If anything hadn't he been giving her space already? Apart from on their night out that was, when they'd got on better than ever. Until the very end anyway.

He didn't want space, damn it. It was the very fact she'd been so keen to get away from him that had made him start to look at what he *did* want. He wanted *her.* The thought of losing her had made him open his eyes.

Finely arched brows disappeared under the waving curtains of her soft hair. 'Say something.'

Quinn frowned harder. What was he supposed to say? There was a danger if he pushed too hard too soon she might run. Maybe if he gave her some space she'd have a chance to miss him, absence and the heart and all that. But what if he'd already left it too late?

It was the most complicated relationship he'd ever been in. But then it was the first one he'd ever wanted to fight for, which was probably why he was behaving so out of character for him…

Clare searched his eyes, and when she spoke her voice was threaded with emotion. '*Please* say something.'

His heart beat erratically; the simple act of breathing in and out became difficult for him. It felt as if he was having his heart dug out of his chest. He couldn't imagine what it would be like not to see her every day. She was tangled up in his life in so many ways. He wanted to hear the soft lilt of her accent, wanted to see the smile that always made him smile back, wanted that hint of light springtime scent as she walked by. He wanted daisies in pots and pens in those holders with dumb pictures of fluffy animals on the front. He wanted to be told off for not being at meetings on time and to be teased when he rebelled.

He searched frantically for a way to tell her all that without backing her into a corner. But she was shaking her head and unfolding her arms…*and moving away from him.*

Quinn had had enough of being someone he wasn't.

One step forward was all it took, and then his fingers were thrusting into her hair, her face was caught between his large palms—and he was kissing her the way he'd wanted to kiss her at her front door. Except that the moment his mouth touched hers all the frustration he'd been feeling shook loose and the kiss became urgent, frenzied, almost desperate. As if he was trying to break through every obstruction that had been in his way to claim her somehow.

Clare rocked back onto her heels under the onslaught, but it was the way she clung to his shoulders, the moans that she made deep in her throat and how she met him halfway with an equal amount of ferocity, that finally broke through the haze.

He moved one hand from her face, snaking his arm down and shifting back enough to allow it space to slide around her waist. Then he drew her in close to where her body fitted against his so perfectly. His fingers flexed against the back of her head, his thumb began a slow smoothing over the soft skin of her cheek. And the kiss changed, slowing by increments until he eventually found a gentleness completely at odds with the passion they'd just shared.

A smile formed on Quinn's lips when her moans became sighs and hums of pleasure that vibrated against his mouth. She had as much fire in her belly as he did, he knew that from the preceding maelstrom, but she was still sweet, gentle Clare. And he wanted to see her—to see how she looked after he'd kissed her.

So he dragged his mouth from hers and looked down into her heavy-lidded eyes. The green was so very dark, her pupils enlarged, and when his gaze dropped she ran the tip of her tongue over her swollen lips. She'd never looked more beautiful.

She would never know what it took to set her away from him. Or how much strength he needed to do what he was about to do.

He stepped back. 'I'll give you a week.'

Clare's eyes widened, her voice one decibel above a whisper. 'What?'

'You wanted space. I'll give you a week.'

She took a swaying step forward. 'Quinn—'

Saying his name so it sounded like a plea didn't help with his resolve, and his voice was terse as a result. 'One week, Clare. Think about what it is you want.' Taking a deep breath, he glanced to his side and then back, lowering and softening his voice so that she understood. 'If this happens there's no going back.'

Pushing. Yes, he knew he was—but he couldn't stop it happening. She needed to understand. He'd tried to fight but it was pointless. Especially after that kiss. If he was going to take his first ever steps out of the land of catch and release and into the unknown universe of catch and keep then she needed to be very sure of what she wanted. There *was* no going back.

Quinn would do everything in his power to make her as addicted to him as he was to her…

If Clare was the culmination of all the dating experiences that had come before her then she was going to reap the benefits of that experience. Quinn had learned who he was. He remembered the women he'd thrown back while waiting for the mythical *one* he'd questioned even existed. What it came down to was that the way Clare had made him feel since he'd opened his eyes had gradually impressed on him the need to keep this one. There had never been anyone like her in his life before and there might never be another. So he was going to fight to keep her.

He'd never been so damn scared in his entire life.

# CHAPTER TEN

CLARE HAD NEVER BEEN so miserable in her entire life.

It was her own stupid fault—she shouldn't have let him walk away. He'd said he didn't want space from her but he'd given it to her in spades. He'd travelled all the way across the flipping country before she'd had time to catch her breath…

'I'm gonna go look at a few places for clubs on the West Coast,' he'd calmly informed her the next morning *over the phone.*

Clare knew he'd toyed with the idea of a place closer to where some of their A-list members lived, and that he'd planned a trip for later in the month. But she knew he'd moved it up. And she knew why. So she'd tried telling him over the phone that she didn't need a week, but he'd cut her off mid-sentence. Apparently since he was the one to set the deadline he was determined both of them would stick to it, whether she liked it or not.

How stupid was he? How could he kiss her like that and then leave? She'd come off the phone hating him. Distancing himself from her hadn't helped her confidence. Especially when he'd left her with the choice between being with him and possibly losing him or not being with him and losing him anyway. Because he was right; there was no going back—they would never be the same ever again.

Twenty-four hours later she'd descended into misery. She missed him so much she couldn't breathe properly. He felt so very far away—and not even in terms of mileage either. She'd never needed to be held so badly in all her life. His solid strength surrounding her—that fresh soap and pure Quinn scent, the feel of his warm breath against her hair and the gravelly edge of his voice sounding in her ears—and if she looked up she'd see the vivid blue of his eyes, and the sinful curve of his mouth would quirk as he tried to hold back a smile…

Another twenty-four hours and she was rapidly spiralling into the realms of tears. So she'd called the cavalry for an afternoon of retail therapy. It had seemed like a good idea at the time.

'Okay, spill.'

She blinked at Erin. 'Spill what?'

'What's going on with you and Quinn?'

Clare scanned the faces of the crowd in the Mexican place they'd found to have lunch off Fifth and Broadway, the fruits of their labours in at least a dozen bags spread at their feet. She didn't want to talk about it, as if part of Quinn's personality had rubbed off on her. She didn't want the whole thing debated, or differing opinions added to the myriad of emotions she was already experiencing. She just wanted him home.

'Can we skip it?'

Erin pushed the remains of her burrito to one side so she could rest her elbows on the table. 'Not when you look like someone just died, no.'

'I really don't want to talk about it.'

Her friends exchanged glances. 'The whole match-making thing opened your eyes, did it?'

'Possibly.' She smiled weakly at Madison, since Madison had asked the question. 'But I really don't want to talk about it.'

'How does he feel?'

Apparently not wanting to talk about it was getting her nowhere. Leaning back, she took a deep breath while she contemplated how Quinn would feel about her talking to the girls about him. Listening to the low mariachi music for a minute, she answered herself: he'd hate it. But desperate times and all that, so she leaned forward again.

'You've known Quinn a lot longer than me, right?'

'Not as long as Morgan and Evan. Why?' They all leaned closer together around the circular table.

'Do you know how he got started in business?'

It obviously wasn't the question they'd been expecting; a look of confusion was exchanged before Erin spoke. 'He already had two of the clubs when I started hanging around with them—I dated one of Morgan's cousins for a while back then…'

Madison shrugged. 'I don't know either…'

Clare frowned and shook her head. 'I swear, it's like some kind of state secret.'

'Does it matter?'

That had been Quinn's theory too, hadn't it? But Clare nodded, because it did; it was a prime example of the kind of things she didn't know about the man she was going to trust with her heart.

Madison continued, 'There's no point asking the guys either—they guard Quinn's privacy like Rottweilers. I don't think he lets that many people get close to him.

It's why everyone was so surprised when he ended up such good friends with you.'

Oh, great. Now she was getting weepy. She could feel her chest tightening, her throat was suddenly raw, and next her eyes would start stinging… The words were making her ache right down to her bones. It wasn't as if Quinn was uncomfortable with people or lacked confidence—in fact he could probably do with a little less of the latter—so why did he hold people at arm's length that way? And, more to the point, why was he still doing it with her?

It was only when a hand squeezed hers again that she realized she'd been staring into nowhere. Her gaze dropped and then followed the arm upwards until she met Erin's eyes.

'Everyone has always wondered what the deal was with you two. Haven't you noticed how many people treat you like a couple already?'

Actually, no, she hadn't. And the idea astounded her. 'Since when? We weren't a couple.'

Madison let the past tense slip by. 'Not in the traditional sense of the word, no. But there's always a fine line between friendship and something more. Didn't you see the way we all reacted the night of the bet? When you made that comment about being a wife in eight out of ten ways we all gasped. It was the first time either of you had ever confronted it. We've been wondering if it would make either of you look at each other differently…'

A little heads-up would have been nice.

'When you think about it, Quinn's been in a relationship with you longer than he's ever been with any other woman.'

Clare had never thought of it that way. It gave her hope, but, she said, 'Doesn't mean I'd make it past the six week cut-off point.'

Erin scowled at her. 'Hey—where's that famous Irish fighting spirit we all love you for, huh?'

Drowning under a quart of ice cream a night—that was where it was. She was going to weigh three hundred pounds by the time Quinn came home. Forcing a smile into place, she took a deep breath, lifted her shoulders and nodded firmly. 'You're right. Let's go and look in the windows at Tiffany's. I'm going to pick a parting gift so expensive it'll bankrupt him.'

They shook their heads in unison, joint smiles negating the admonishment Madison aimed her way. 'Stop that. If he breaks your heart he'll have us to deal with.'

A week was seven days too long for Quinn. He'd known there was no way he was sticking to it, so he'd put himself on a plane. Even if he hadn't been feeling the need to bang his head against a brick wall for that genius idea he couldn't have stayed away the full seven days. Not while he missed Clare the way he did…

By day three, having dutifully looked over all the potential real estate, he decided enough was enough.

Her time was up. So when another summer day had come and gone away in an eternally sunny Los Angeles he booked a flight home. It didn't matter what she'd decided, he was going home and he was going to launch a charm offensive. He liked that plan much better. It wasn't backing her into a corner. Not the way he had by giving her an ultimatum in the first place. Granted, it wasn't giving her the space she'd asked for either, but tough. By giving her space he'd taken a chance she might form a list of reasons not to get involved with him…

The thought made his need to get home more urgent than before. So by the time he got out of a yellow cab in front of his house—when he should have been bone tired after three nights without sleep and an eight hour flight—he was edgy, restless and frustrated beyond belief that he couldn't just go knock on her door. But it was late—he couldn't go and wake her up just so he could start seducing her, could he? Slow and steady won the race, they said. Whoever they might be…

One of the worst things Clare had endured since Quinn had left was insomnia. It was getting to the stage where she felt like the walking dead. So for the third night in a row she groaned loudly in frustration and threw the light covers off her body before swinging her legs over the edge of the bed and sitting up.

She glanced at the blue digital readout on her alarm clock—half past midnight—so that meant she'd been tossing and turning and feigning sleep for two hours. And she'd tried watching a movie, she'd tried reading a book—heck, she'd even tried some of the relaxation techniques she'd learnt in the handful of yoga classes she'd taken with Madison and Erin back in January, when they'd all said it was time to try something new.

But nothing had worked.

She made her way into the kitchen and poured a glass of water, then rinsed the glass, set it on the side and turned to open the French windows. It had been horrifically humid all day long, something the Irish girl in her still found it hard to adjust to. So when she stepped barefoot onto the lawn the fine mist of rain that appeared was almost a godsend.

Closing her eyes, she leaned back, lifting her arms wide and letting the lukewarm spray sprinkle down on her face. Then she turned slowly on her heels, feeling the grass between her toes and breathing a deep lungful of damp air. Actually, it felt quite good.

Now if the aching would just go away—if the part of her that felt as if it was missing could just be returned to her—if she just didn't hurt *so very much...* The next deep breath she took shuddered through her entire body; if he would just *come home...*

Then she could show him, literally, that space was the last thing she wanted.

Dumping his bags in the hall, Quinn walked through the darkness to the kitchen at the back of the house, not needing light to see where he was going. What he should do was go and run off the varying methods of seduction his imagination had decided to supply while repeating the words *slow and steady* until his body got the message.

The dim light from the house next door's motion-sensitive security lighting cast long shadows on the floor from the windows, where a fine mist of rain was frosting the glass. He'd gone running in worse. If he went running it would maybe help with the deep-seated need to go downstairs.

He hesitated in the middle of the room, unsure why he'd gone in there in the first place.

He wasn't going downstairs, but he wondered what she was doing. It was after midnight so she was probably asleep. Was she wearing what she'd been wearing the night he'd sat outside her window? Did she own any of the sexy things she'd talked about on the phone that night?

Okay—now he *really* needed to go for a run—and possibly a cold shower…

Yanking his jacket off, he stepped over to the French windows to throw it over the back of a chair. At first he had to blink a couple of times to be sure he was seeing what he was seeing. Once he'd convinced himself he wasn't seeing her simply because he wanted to see her so badly he smiled at what she was doing. What *was* she doing? Was she crazy? His heart didn't think it was crazy—his heart thought it was exactly the kind of unexpected and uniquely endearing thing Clare *would* do. Joy in the simple things, right?

Only Clare…only *his* Clare…

She focused hard on her breathing while she continued turning, forcing the need to cry—again—back down inside. It was all about control after all. And she really needed to get it under control before she saw Quinn again.

Tilting her outstretched arms from side to side like a child making impressions of an aeroplane, she leaned her head from shoulder to shoulder and smiled sadly at the sudden need for the comfort of childish games. She bent her knees, crossed one leg over the other and turned a little faster, resisting the urge to make aeroplane *noises* too—but only just. The buzzing when a child pressed its lips together to get the engine noise had always made her smile too.

When she tried the turn a second time she stumbled, arms dropping and eyes opening as she chuckled at her own ridiculousness—she really was losing her mind—and it was then she looked up and saw him standing on the edge of the patio…

The world tilted beneath her feet. Quinn smiled the most amazingly gorgeous, slow, sexy smile at her and her heart flipped over in her chest in response.

He was *home.*

When he dropped his chin and his expression held a hint of uncertainty, joy bubbled up inside her.

She breathed out the words. 'You're home.'

'I'm home,' the gruff-edged voice she loved so much replied. 'Miss me?'

Clare felt her eyes welling up, her throat tight so the most she could manage was to nod frantically.

She saw him exhale—as if he'd been holding his breath until he got her reply—and his voice was even gruffer than before. 'How much?'

When her heart stopped, her feet grew wings. She was across the lawn and flinging herself into his waiting arms before she'd allowed herself time to second-guess what she was doing. Then, with her arms around the thick column of his neck, her cheek against his, she laughed joyously as he lifted her off her feet; groaning against her ear. '*Good*—cos *I* missed *you.*'

She leaned back to look into his sensational eyes. 'How much?'

Quinn examined her eyes for a long moment before informing her. 'Okay, you better know what it is you want, O'Connor. This is your ten second warning.'

Clare smiled uncontrollably at him, wriggling her toes in the air. 'My what?'

'Ten-second warning.' He nodded the tiniest amount, his deep voice intimately low as it rumbled up from his chest. The vibration filtered through their layers of clothing to tickle her overly sensitive breasts. 'In ten seconds I'm going to kiss you. So that's how long you have to stop me…'

Clare stared at him in wonder, sure that any minute she was going to awaken and end up miserable again because she'd dreamed what was happening.

His chest expanded. 'Ten…nine…eight…'

She ducked down and pressed her mouth to his.

His lips were warm and firm, and for a long moment he froze, allowing her to tentatively explore their shape. But when her lips parted and she added pressure he moved with her, the kiss soft and gentle and so very tender that it touched her soul. It felt as if the part of her that had been missing was being returned with each slide of his mouth over hers. She could kiss and be kissed by him for days on end. She really could.

Moving her hands, she let her fingertips brush against the short spikes of his cropped hair while she breathed his scent in deep. And then she caught his lower lip between her teeth in a light nip, and smiled against his mouth when he groaned low down in his chest, the sound more empowering than anything she'd ever experienced.

Letting her feet swing from side to side, her body brushing back and forth against his with the movement, she smiled all the more when the sound in his chest became a groan, his words vibrating against her lips. 'Are nice Irish girls supposed to kiss like this?'

Clare lifted her head enough to change angles. 'Maybe I'm not as nice as you like to think I am.'

'Hmmm.' The sound buzzed her sensitive lips in the exact way the aeroplane noise would have if she'd made it. The thought made laughter bubble effervescently inside her. 'I wasn't complaining…'

He moved one arm, keeping her suspended off the ground as if she weighed nothing while his free hand rose to thread long fingers into her hair. And then he cradled the back of her head in his palm and deepened the kiss—stealing the air from her lungs and making her feel vaguely light-headed.

Clare couldn't have said how long they kissed for; she didn't even realize he was gently swinging her from side to side until he began a slow circling to go with it. And it made her wonder how long he'd been standing watching her turning circles on the lawn—what he was doing was a more sensual version of what she'd been doing alone.

Using the hand in her hair to draw her back a little, so he could look at her when she finally lifted her heavy eyelids, his eyes glowed as Clare smiled drunkenly at him.

'Hello, you.'

Clare's heart swelled. 'Hello, you.'

She looked over her shoulder when he started carrying her across the patio and down the steps, turned to look at him again as they got close to her doors. The disappointment evident in her voice, she asked, 'Are we stopping kissing now?'

'Like hell we are.'

The firm reply made her wiggle her toes again while she openly studied his face.

'Forgot what I looked like, did you?'

'You were gone a very long time. I'm just checking nothing has changed.'

In front of her large sofa, he let her slide oh, so

slowly, down the length of his body, until her feet touched the floor. Then he sat down, tugging her onto his lap before leaning over until she was lying on her back looking up at him.

Quinn's hand rose, and he watched as his fingertips smoothed her hair back before beginning a slow exploration of her face, his gaze rising to tangle with hers while he traced her lips. 'Something has changed.'

She knew he didn't mean their faces. 'It did—a while back.'

He nodded, lowering his gaze to watch in wonder as he brushed his thumb back and forth over her lower lip. 'One step at a time, okay?'

'Okay.' She lifted a hand and framed the side of his face, the small sigh and the lowering of his thick lashes to half-mast telling her everything she needed to know for now. 'I need you to talk to me, though, Quinn.'

He took a deeper breath. 'You might need to work with me on that. It's new ground.'

'I know.' Smiling softly, she moved her hand around to the back of his head and drew him towards her. 'Where were we?'

Thick lashes lifted again, his thumb moving to the corner of her mouth. 'Here.'

He kissed where his thumb had been, then lifted his head an inch and moved his thumb over her bottom lip to the other corner. 'And here.'

Clare didn't care how late it was, or that they both had work to think about when the sun came up—it didn't matter; the new day could wait. When she was eventually lying across him, with her head tucked beneath his chin, she lifted her chin enough to whisper up at him. 'Stay.'

'Here?'

'Right here.' She snuggled back into place, her palm resting against the steady beat of his heart. 'I haven't been sleeping so good.'

His arms tightened. 'Me either.'

'So stay.'

'Just so long as you still respect me in the morning.' He reached up for the throw rug she had tossed over the back of the sofa.

'Well, I don't know about that one…'

Lethargy settled over her as he smoothed his hand in circles against her back. 'Do you trust me, Clare?'

'You know I do.'

'You know I'd never do anything to hurt you?'

'I know.'

'But you know I'm not easy?'

She smiled sleepily. 'Spoken by the man sleeping over after our second kiss.'

'I need you to know what you're getting into. I'm not—'

'I know what I'm getting into. You said a while back that I knew enough. And I do.'

When he continued smoothing his hand over her back she felt herself drawn down into the depths of the kind of languorous sleep she hadn't experienced since he'd left; still smiling as she did.

She was going to give that six week deadline of his a run for its money…

# CHAPTER ELEVEN

'DISCO BABIES?'

Quinn smiled from his perch on the edge of her desk as she pushed the filing cabinet shut with her hip and turned to look at him with enthusiasm dancing in her eyes. 'Yes. Parents bring their kids along and they all dance together and have a great time. It wouldn't take much to get it going. And it doesn't interfere with what you already do.'

It wasn't that he didn't think it was a good idea. He did. He just liked having Clare persuade him that it was.

When she attempted to get past he casually reached out, hooking an arm around her waist and spreading his legs to make room for her. She didn't put up a fight—she never did. Instead her hands slid over his shoulders and linked together at the back of his neck, her thumbs massaging the base of his skull so he automatically leaned back into the touch.

'You want to turn my clubs into kids' playgrounds?'

'No-o.' She smiled when he splayed his fingers on her hips. 'I want you to consider how much money parents spend, especially in a city with lots of rich parents…'

Quinn nodded. 'Uh-huh. It has nothing to do with the sight of all those dancing babies? The cute card isn't swaying you any?'

'You *like* this idea.' She turned her face a little to the side and quirked her brow knowingly. 'You know you do.'

It never ceased to amaze him how much her confidence seemed to have grown since they'd started dating for real. She'd blossomed before his very eyes. Not that she hadn't been something before—but now?

Well, now she was *something*.

And Quinn had real problems keeping his hands off her. For someone who'd never been renowned for being overly demonstrative in public, he'd gone through quite a transformation of late. He was holding her hand as they walked through Manhattan, kissing her at hotdog stands in Times Square, and randomly grinning like an idiot even when she wasn't there. She was shooting his reputation for cool, detached control down in flames. The thing was, he liked it that she was.

'It has possibilities.'

'See.' She sidled closer and leaned him back over the desk, her long lashes lowering as she focused her gaze on his mouth. 'I knew you'd like it. I'm getting much better at discovering things you *like*...'

Smiling at the innuendo, he removed one hand from her hip to brace his palm on the desk, lifting his chin. 'You think you have me all figured out now, don't you?'

'Oh, I still have a few secrets to discover; keeps you interesting, mind you...'

The thought of her finding out everything before he told her himself made his smile fade, and Clare immediately searched his eyes and saw what must have been a flash of doubt. Her voice softened in response.

'And I've told you a few million times now that nothing will change how I see you.'

With each passing week Quinn liked to believe that was true, but he'd wanted her to be more attached to him before he took the chance. The way he figured it, it was just a case of making sure she was insanely crazy about him first. With that in mind, he sat upright to bring his nose within an inch of hers, his fingers curling into her hair.

Angling his head, he examined her eyes up close, blinking lazily. 'Bring me any ideas involving pets and my clubs and we may need to have a serious talk.'

When a smile formed in her eyes he closed the gap and kissed her long and slow, until the hands at his nape unlocked and gripped onto his shoulders and she rocked forwards, pressing her breasts in tight against his chest. She was temptation personified. Resisting her was getting to be nigh on impossible. Slow and steady was a mammoth test of his endurance.

Quinn moved the hand on her hip around to her back, slipping it under the edge of her blouse so he could touch his fingertips to baby-soft skin. The fooling around they'd been doing had been escalating of late, and it couldn't happen soon enough as far as Quinn was concerned. He had only to think about touching her and his reaction was so strong and so fierce that it left his body in an almost constant state of pain.

She knew it too—the witch. Good little Irish girl, his eye. She'd been pushing him closer and closer to the edge for weeks.

When he slid his hand further up she made a muffled sound of complaint against his mouth and wriggled. 'Don't you dare.'

When she lifted her head he feigned nonchalance. 'Dare what?'

'You know what.' When she tried to wriggle free he dropped his hand from her hair and used the arm to circle her waist and keep her still. Clare laughed throatily in response. 'I swear if you undo that before my client arrives you're in big, big trouble.'

With a flick of his thumb and forefinger he unhooked her bra. Her hands immediately lifted to hold the material in place—cupping her breasts. 'I *hate* that you can do that.'

Quinn grinned. 'Old high school party piece.'

'Too much information, Casanova.' She mock scowled at him, her eyes dancing with amusement. *'Fix it.'*

'Say please.'

'Fix it or I'm telling Morgan and Evan you bring me daisies twice a week…'

'Yes, because my ability to charm you is something I should be ashamed of—obviously.'

'Fix it.' She leaned closer to whisper in his ear. 'Or I'm telling them you watched *Breakfast at Tiffany's* and *enjoyed it.*'

Okay, that one would run and run, so he placed a kiss on the sensitive skin below her ear before lifting both hands under her blouse to fix what he'd done. 'I might have to stop being nice to you.'

Truthfully, he probably wouldn't have enjoyed the movie as much if she hadn't loved every minute of it. But then that was something else that had crept up on him: his state of happiness being directly related to hers. The fact that when she smiled he smiled had always been there, even when they were friends—but it was so much more than that now. Some days he even wondered if all the touching they did had led to her emotions being transmitted to him.

Quinn grimaced at the effort it took not to laugh when she wiggled about, making sure everything was back in place. His voice was filled with husky-edged amusement. 'Can I help you with that?'

'No—you can go away. You have a meeting in fifteen minutes.'

'I have another ten minutes, then, don't I?'

'Like heck you do.' But she smiled at him anyway, leaning in for another kiss. 'Go.'

Quinn sighed heavily. 'Maybe for the best. There's someone confused enough by the writing on the doors to be one of your clients.'

When he jerked his head in the direction of the doors Clare turned and smiled encouragingly at the woman before glaring back at Quinn. 'How do you *do that*?'

He shrugged. 'I have amazingly good eyes.'

The woman pushed the door open just as Quinn let Clare loose, the turn of her body giving him enough cover to slide his fingers over the curve of her rear as he stood and walked past. When she jumped a little he smiled, leaned in and shook the woman's hand,

'Hi, there—I'm gonna leave you girls to talk romance, and Clare will fix you right up.' He winked. 'She has excellent taste in men.'

The woman smiled back. 'If she has a few more like you on her books I'll be more than happy…'

'Why, thank you.' He inclined his head, glancing at Clare in time to see her roll her eyes. 'But I'm afraid I'm temporarily out of circulation.'

The woman laughed girlishly while Quinn walked

towards the door, turning on his heel to walk the last few steps backwards so he could point a long finger at Clare over her client's head. 'Don't be late tonight.'

She made a small snort of derision. 'I'm not the one who's normally late for things.' She tapped her wrist-watch with meaning. 'Would you go away, you clown? I'm going to find Marilyn the man of her dreams.'

Marilyn grinned at Clare when Quinn left. 'Boy-friend, I take it?'

It was the first time she'd been asked the question, and Clare hesitated on the answer. Telling the woman in front of her he was her boss would seem strange after the interchange she'd just witnessed. Boyfriend, however, suggested that it was something committed, and even though every bone in Clare's body ached for that kind of stability with Quinn she was still deeply aware of the fact they were in his usual honeymoon period. If she got past the six-week cut-off point she'd probably feel better…

One week to go…

It didn't stop her wanting to say it out loud, just the once while he couldn't hear her, as if saying it would make it more real.

'Yes.' For now anyway…

'He's gorgeous.'

He played on it no end too, the brat. But she was so completely wrapped up in him she couldn't call him on it. Everything was so *right* in so many ways. She'd honestly never been happier. It was why she'd decided to seduce him. Sometimes a girl had to do what a girl had to do. Not that she'd ever set out to seduce a man before, or had the faintest idea how to go about it with a man like Quinn. But they'd been fooling around long enough for her to have a fair idea of what worked and what didn't…

Linking arms with Marilyn, she guided her towards the seating area. 'Let's see if we can find you someone just as gorgeous, shall we?'

Someone Marilyn could love as much as Clare loved Quinn. Because she did; she'd probably been falling for him long before she'd realized it. The slow build had led to a deeper emotion than she'd ever felt before. It made the relationship she'd had with Jamie look shallow and pointless in comparison. But then Clare supposed there was no way to know if what you felt was real until the real thing arrived. *You just know*, they said. They were right. Clare just knew.

She was head over heels in love with Quinn. And he now had the ability to hurt her as she'd never been hurt before…

'Where are we going?'

'We're here. Close your eyes.'

'If I close my eyes how can I see where we are?' She cocked a brow in challenge.

'In the future when you complain about a lack of surprises can we remember how bad you are with them?'

The very mention of the word future was enough to earn a firm kiss, her arm lifting to wrap around his neck. 'But we're already here. All you have to do is yell "surprise."'

Quinn smiled indulgently as the door behind her was opened by their driver. 'You have to promise you'll close your eyes in the elevator when I say so.'

Intrigued, Clare slid across the soft white leather and swung her knees out. Lifting her head when she was on the sidewalk, she blinked at her surroundings, smiling when Quinn's fingers tangled with hers.

'The Rockefeller Centre? Isn't it closed at this time of night?'

Quinn leaned his face close to hers, his gaze fixed forward as he stage whispered in her ear, 'Not when you have the means to keep it open, no.'

They walked past the row of United Nations flags, Clare's eyes automatically seeking out the Irish one so she could smile its way. Then she looked at the golden statue of Prometheus and the art deco buildings surrounding them before she turned towards Quinn and lifted her chin.

'So what are we doing this time?'

The night had started with a limo at her door, progressing to a sell-out Broadway show and supper at one of the chicest restaurants in Manhattan, leaving Clare feeling distinctly like royalty.

Quinn chuckled, his smile lighting up his vivid eyes. 'Wait and see.'

She decided she liked champagne and caviar dates if he got so much enjoyment out of them. Not that she needed them every day, because she didn't. She was just as happy with a hotdog stand in Times Square, or sitting on the steps outside the house they shared eating bagels in the early morning after his run, or lying across the sofa watching a movie late at night…

But Quinn had excelled himself. She barely had words when they finally stepped out of the elevator at the Top of the Rock and he uncovered her eyes. The panoramic view of New York at night spread endlessly before her.

Hand in hand they walked to the edge, and she took

in everything from the Chrysler Building lit up in green through to the Empire State Building with its ethereal glow of white light. It was breathtaking.

'Over here.'

When she turned she saw what she'd missed: a small table set for two—candles flickering inside glass globes—smiling daisies in a vase. It was perfect.

Squeezing his fingers, she pressed into his side, her voice filled with awe. 'How did you do this?'

Quinn smiled lazily, his gravelly voice low. 'One of the joys of dating a rich guy.'

The very fact he'd spent what must have amounted to a small fortune to hire the place after hours—*for her*—made her want to tell him there and then how much she loved him.

'You don't have to impress me on a date any more, you know. I'm a sure thing.'

He stopped at the side of the table, turned and wrapped the fingers of his free hand around the nape of her neck, his thumb tilting her chin up so he could kiss her before mumbling against her lips. 'Sure thing, huh?'

She bobbed her head. And was rewarded with another kiss before he stepped back, freeing his hands so he could lift a silver dome from a plate. 'Caviar…'

Clare chuckled at his theatrics as he jerked his head towards the table. 'Champagne, naturally…'

'You've never actually done a champagne and caviar date before, have you?'

'Never let it be said I can't rise to a challenge.'

'This cost you a small fortune, didn't it?'

Wide shoulders jerked. 'Not all of it…'

Naturally it made her look at the table again. 'What's under the other dome?'

'Good of you to ask.' He reached forward. 'Didn't know how you felt about fish eggs…so…'

When he revealed the other plate she laughed. 'Apple pie, perchance?'

'Apple pie.' He grinned. 'Best of both worlds.'

'You hate fish eggs, don't you?'

'Can't stand them.'

She took the dome from his hand and set it down before insinuating herself under his jacket and wrapping her arms around his lean waist. 'Okay. So the apple pie would be for whom, exactly?'

'I figured we could share.'

'Sharing works for me. Did you bring ice cream?' Not that she had so much of a need for it any more.

'I did.' He leaned down and pressed a row of kisses up the side of her neck before whispering in her ear. 'Rocky road…'

'You thought of everything.'

Quinn kissed back down her neck, nuzzling into the indentation of her collarbone before surprising her by releasing her. 'Well, as it happens…'

When the haunting strains of 'Moon River' sounded over the whisper of city noises in the wind, emotion rose in a wave inside her, her voice wavering as a result.

'The *Breakfast at Tiffany's* music…'

He nodded, his gaze fixed on hers as he slowly made his way back around the table. 'Can't have you thinking I don't pay attention to the little details, can I?'

Heaven help her, he'd be like that as a lover too, wouldn't he? Clare knew it as instinctively as her body knew to breathe in and out. Never, ever had she wanted a man as badly as she wanted Quinn; all the patience he'd been exercising not to push her into sleeping with him was driving her crazy. How could he not know that?

He stepped backwards, drawing her into an open space before he wrapped his arm around her waist. When she lifted a hand to his shoulder and brought her hips in against his he began to sway them—oh, so slowly—and the softness in the vivid blue of his eyes was enough to bring tears to the backs of hers.

'Do I get to graduate from the school of dating etiquette yet?'

Clare had to clear her throat to answer. 'With flying colours.'

'Good.'

When he celebrated by whirling her in circles before dipping her backwards to kiss her breathless she looked up at him with dancing eyes.

'Where did you learn to dance?'

Dark brows waggled at her as he drew her upright and back against his body. 'My mother insisted all the Cassidy boys knew the basics. The dip and kiss I added.'

'Remind me to thank her when I see her.'

'And have her rub it in that she was right? I think not.'

Clare smiled softly. 'Anything else I don't know about that you want to tell me?'

The expression on his face changed in a heartbeat. 'Yes. There's a lot.'

She lifted her brows in question.

Quinn took a shallow breath and looked over her head. 'You asked me how I got started with the clubs.'

Clare kept her voice low in case she broke the spell. 'On the door, right?'

'Yes.' He frowned. 'But that's not how I ended up

buying the first one. I could never have afforded it on the wages I earned.'

'Okay.'

Thick lashes flickered as he watched a fine lock of her hair catch in the breeze. 'My old man left a life insurance policy. For a lot more than anyone thought he could; he couldn't stick to much of anything else, but somehow he kept up the payments on it his whole life…'

'He left it to you?'

'No, but I'd pretty much been the provider for the family since I turned sixteen—worked construction sites during the day—so my mother trusted me to put it to good use. When I talked about trying to get a mortgage for the club after it came up for sale, she staked me. I paid it back with interest.'

Why on earth hadn't he felt he could tell her that?

'He'd have been very proud of you, your dad.'

It was the wrong thing to say. She knew it the second his mouth twisted. 'He wouldn't have given a damn. It'd been twelve years since he bothered with his family. Dying and leaving the money was the best thing he ever did for any of us.'

The bitterness in his words sent a shiver up Clare's spine. 'I thought he died when you were little?'

Quinn frowned at her. 'Who told you that?'

'No one.' She floundered. 'I just—well, when you said about that fight you had—your nickname—'

His eyes widened. 'You thought I got into that fight to defend him?'

'Well, yes. Sort of. I thought—'

'Every word they said about him that day was true. What made me see red was the fact they said I was just like him. Apple never falls far from the tree, or words to that effect. The truth can hurt more than anything else…' He took a deep breath, held it for a moment, and pursed his lips into a thin line before continuing. 'I didn't want to be told I was like him. Problem is, I'm the walking image of him—the young version of him anyway. I see him in the mirror every day.'

Clare's eyes searched his, catching sight of an inner torture that made her ache for him. It made her fearful of knowing everything she'd wanted to know. But she knew what it meant for Quinn to let her in, so she asked the question. 'What did he do?'

'He was a drunk. A lousy one.' His arms tightened before he added the one thing he had to know Clare would feel the deepest. 'And he cheated on my mom from before I was born.'

Clare gasped, feeling the pain as keenly for his mother as she ever had for herself, maybe more. She'd met Quinn's mother countless times and adored her. She was one of the strongest, warmest, most caring women Clare had ever met. From the moment Clare had arrived in New York with Jamie—feeling more than a little lost and overwhelmed—Maggie Cassidy had made it her business to ensure she felt welcomed into their community. When Jamie had left she'd been the first to come and see her. Not once had she ever let on that she understood better than most how Clare had felt.

She shook her head, trying to make sense of it. 'But she had more kids with him. They must have—'

'Thought having each of those kids would save their marriage? They probably did. But it didn't. She put up with him for years, because she remembered what he'd been like when she fell for him. And she let him convince her time and time again that he could change. But he didn't change.' Quinn paused. 'He got worse.'

'My God.' Clare breathed the words at him. 'Is that why you were so worried I might think you were like Jamie? You thought because your father was a cheater…'

Was *that* why he never stayed in a relationship more than six weeks? Did he think if he even looked at another woman there was a chance he might stray, so rather than hurt anyone he cut them loose? It was a twisted logic, but it made sense.

Quinn's voice was fiercely determined. 'I may look like my old man, but…'

Clare slid her hand off his neck and framed his face, smoothing the harsh line at one side of his mouth with her thumb while she told him in an equally determined voice, 'You're talking about genetics, Quinn—not who you are inside. I *know* you.'

But he removed her hand from his face. 'For a long time I was more like my old man than I wanted to be. We're taught that growing up, people like you and me—aren't we? It's the Irish thing. We're taught how it runs through us, how it's part of who we are; the generations that went before run in our veins.'

'Yes, but not the way you—'

Just when she feared he was distancing himself from her, he caught her fingers in his and squeezed tight. 'I listened to that when I was a kid. I thought that his blood running through my veins and looking like him meant I'd end up exactly the same. I've spent a good portion of my life proving I'm not.'

He smiled a smile that didn't make it all the way up into his eyes. 'But I certainly had his temper. And that day in the playground showed me I could be just as quick with my fists.'

Clare's chest cramped so badly she could barely catch her breath—*no.* 'He didn't…?'

His gravelly voice said the words she didn't want to hear. 'Like I said—lousy drunk.'

'Oh, *Quinn.*'

*Not her Quinn.* Her eyes filled with tears. It all made sense to her now. He hadn't been able to defend himself against a grown up, but all the anger and hurt he'd felt had been directed at five boys his own age when they'd told him he was exactly like the man who'd caused him that pain. It wasn't *fair.*

Quinn smoothed his hand down her back. 'It only happened the one time. My mom had us all packed and moved to Brooklyn before it could happen again.'

Blinking the tears away, Clare found the strength to lift her chin. 'I'd have done the same thing.'

'I like to hope you'd have left sooner.' He smiled with his eyes before his mouth quirked. 'You're stronger than you give yourself credit for, O'Connor. I saw it that day when you had to go face those people and tell them there was no wedding. I don't think I've ever respected anyone more than I respected you that day.'

Untangling her fingers from his, she lifted both hands to the tensed muscles of his shoulders, shaking him firmly as she informed him, 'Listen up, Quinn Cassidy. You're *not* him. I know that. You know that. And you could have told me all of this any time and it wouldn't *ever* have changed how I see you. Nothing you do or say could change how I feel about you. I—'

The words were almost out before he interrupted her. 'I hope you mean that.'

'*Quinn!*' How could he think—?

'No, you need to know.' He took a breath, and then said the words that literally stopped her heart.

'I sent Jamie away that day.'

# CHAPTER TWELVE

WHAT QUINN HAD SAID didn't make any sense to her. But as she searched his eyes she automatically stepped back, frowning when he set her fingers free, almost as if he'd known she would need space and been prepared for it.

'I don't understand. Why—?'

'Someone had to do something.' She saw a muscle clench in his jaw. 'I guess it was always gonna be me.'

*'Someone?'* He made it sound like—

Her brows jerked. 'Everyone *knew*?'

'That he was messing around? Yes. He didn't make much of a secret of it. He never did. He was one of the best friends I ever had, but on that one subject we never agreed; he was a player for as long as I knew him.'

*Everyone knew?* Having the man she'd followed blindly across an ocean cheat on her was bad enough on its own, but that everyone had known, and had no doubt been talking about it while she'd sailed through her fantasy bubble days blissfully unaware, was too much. It was like being slapped. She'd walked out there in front of all those people and they'd *known*—

She felt nauseous. 'You *all* knew and none of you thought to tell *me*?'

The sense of betrayal was overwhelming.

'It caused more arguments than we'd ever had before. But when it came down to it we didn't know you that well, and no one wanted to be the one to cause you that much pain. So I dealt with Jamie. *Him* I knew.'

'Draw the short straw did you?'

She saw anger flash in his eyes. *'No.'*

'Well, what then?' She flung an arm out to her side, humiliation morphing rapidly into anger. 'Because you're leader of the pack it was your job to fix things for the poor wee Irish girl?'

When he stepped closer she lifted her hands to his chest to push him away, but he grasped them in his and held on. 'Go ahead and let it out, O'Connor. Yell, shout, call me all the names you want. But I'd do it again.'

'You patronising, self-righteous…' She laughed a little hysterically, tugging on her hands. 'Let me go.'

He held on. 'I know you're hurt—'

'*Hurt?* Oh, hurt doesn't even begin to cover how I feel right this minute. I thought I'd made some real friends here—people I could *trust.*' She tugged again.

He still held on, looking down at her with an air of self-composure that made her want to lash out. To say things that would make him hurt as much as she did. Anything that might make him understand how much she hated him for bursting the bubble of happiness she'd allowed herself to inhabit—*again.* It wasn't that she saw him differently or loved him less; it was just that she was so very—

*Hurt.*

Just as he'd said—but she couldn't back down and tell him that. She didn't want to. He had to have known what telling her would make her feel. Why tell her now?

Why, when it was all behind her, had he felt she needed to know?

Was it a way to make her hate him before he handed her a little blue box? But that didn't make any sense. Why set up such an incredible night and open up to her the way he had if he planned on cutting her loose?

But she ignored reason, unable to focus anywhere beyond putting the final pieces of the puzzle together. 'What did you do, exactly? I want all of it.'

When he grimaced she tugged harder to free herself, stumbling back a step when he let go and said her name with a pleading tone. *'Clare—'*

'No—come on—you were so determined I needed to know, so tell me. What did you do? What did you say to plead my case for me? To try and get him to stay with me when he so very obviously didn't want to?'

Quinn's eyes flashed. 'He should never have brought you here!'

Clare flinched. So much for what he'd said about her making the right decision to stay, then. She nodded, biting hard on her lower lip as she began to pace aimlessly. 'Right. I don't belong here. Good to know.'

Quinn swore viciously. 'That's not what I meant. I meant he should never have brought you here when he had no intention of staying faithful to you. You deserved better. I told him that.'

She nodded again. 'And how long after I arrived did you tell him that?'

When he didn't answer she stopped pacing, the set of Quinn's shoulders and the clench of his jaw telling her he was fighting a silent battle.

*'How long?'*

His gaze locked with hers. 'A month.'

Wow, the truth really did hurt. To know she'd managed to hold her fiancé's attention for less than a whole month was a real kick in the guts. Even knowing he was lower than a snake's behind didn't help how bruised her confidence felt.

Dropping her head back, she blinked at the sky as she tried to control her anger, her gaze flickering back and forth while her mind searched for answers to what it was she'd apparently been lacking.

Quinn's voice softened, sounding closer. 'It wasn't anything you did or didn't do. It was him. He was a fool, Clare—I told him *that* too.'

'So basically you warned him off. Did what—? Threatened to tell me what he was doing?' She laughed as she dropped her chin and looked at him. 'Bit of an empty threat that one, wasn't it?'

'What was I supposed to do? Drop in for coffee and just land it in your lap? I didn't know you well enough for that. It was none of my business.'

'You *made it* your business!'

'Yes.' He nodded brusquely. 'I *did.* Someone had to. Up till then I was his closest friend, so I told him straight what he was doing was wrong. I gave him a chance to make it right. He owed you that.'

Clare still didn't get it. Quinn was right about many things; it hadn't been any of his business, she'd meant nothing to him back then—hell, he'd barely given her the time of day. Why would he take her part against someone who'd been one of his best friends for years?

Her eyes widened with horror. 'Tell me you didn't run him off because *you* wanted me.'

Rage arrived so fast she felt it travel through the air like a shockwave. *'What?'*

'It's what *he* did, you know.' She nodded. 'I was seeing someone—just casually, mind you—but we'd been dating for a couple of weeks until Jamie came along and launched his charm offensive. He used to joke that he stole me away, that it took strategy and a long term plan. Did *you* have a long term plan, Quinn? Is that what *this* is? I remember what Morgan used to say about you and Jamie always competing for the girls in high school. He said you were always rivals when it came to women.'

Quinn bunched his hands into fists at his sides. 'I'm back to being slime again, am I? I stepped up because what he was doing to you was *wrong*! He was about to make a commitment to you—a lifetime commitment. Not only did he make the promises to you, he dragged you all the way over here—away from your family and your friends—and then after you'd given up so much to be with him he...'

He had to pause for breath, turning his face away while he fought to keep his anger in check. Clare read every sign, knew everything he'd said was true. It was that honourable streak of his—it was his belief in right and wrong and his ability to care about the welfare of others...

They were all part of the man she'd fallen so deeply in love with. He'd championed her, hadn't he? In that old-fashioned knight in shining armour way that women dreamed of.

*She just wished she'd known.* 'You should have told me.'

When he looked at her with an expression of raw agony the very foundations of their relationship shook beneath her feet. When tears formed in her eyes, she wrapped her arms tight around her waist to hold the agony inside, her voice barely above a whisper.

'You offered me the job and a place to stay out of guilt, didn't you?'

Even the words left a bitter taste in her mouth. Their entire relationship was based on a lie. How could they ever come back from that?

'Clare, please—'

*'Didn't you?'* Her voice cracked.

'At the beginning, yes—partly…' He swallowed hard, and the fact that he was so hesitant broke her in two. 'He humiliated you publicly and left you in debt, but you loved it here. You needed a job and I had one. Then you needed a place to stay—and I had one. It made sense.'

Quinn stepped into her line of vision, her gaze immediately focusing on a random button on his shirt before working its way up, button by button…

'But, yes, I did feel guilty about what happened. I told Jamie to fight for what he had with you or leave. I had no idea he would wait till your wedding day to make a decision. If I had I wouldn't have let it happen. When it did I told him never to come back.'

Clare's gaze lingered on the sweep of his mouth before searching out the slight bump on the ridge of his nose, her voice suddenly flat. 'I bet you didn't say it as calmly as that.'

'No, I didn't.'

She nodded, somehow finding the strength to look into the reflected light shimmering in the dark pools of his eyes. 'Did you hit him?'

Out of nowhere she remembered the smudges of dirt on his suit when he'd come to tell her Jamie was gone. And when he sighed deeply she had her answer.

So she nodded again. 'Saved me doing it, I guess.'

'We said a lot of other stuff too; it got personal—and heated. We hadn't been seeing eye to eye on a lot of things even before you came on the scene.'

Because Jamie had been a player, and a man of honour like Quinn would have had problems with that. Clare got it now. If she'd known Jamie as well as Quinn had, she'd never have followed him to the States to begin with. But then she'd never have met Quinn…

She dragged her gaze from his eyes and looked out into the distance. 'Maybe you're right; I should never have come over here to begin with.'

'You belong here now.'

When she shook her head, the never-ending panorama of twinkling lights beyond the edges of the building blurred in front of her eyes and her lower lip trembled. 'I thought I did.'

'You *do*. This is your home.' His fingertips brushed against her cheek. 'You belong with—'

Clare's breath caught on a sob as she moved her face out of his reach. 'Don't. Please. Not now.'

From the fog of her peripheral vision she saw his hand drop. 'Don't ask me for space, Clare. I mean it. I didn't want to give it to you last time.'

Sharply turning her head, she frowned hard. 'So I'm supposed to do what? Pretend I'm fine with all this and just let it go?'

'I'm not asking you to do that either.'

'Then *what is it* you expect me to do?'

'Work through it with me!' His large hands rose to frame her face so fast she didn't have time to step away. Then he stepped in, towering over her and lowering his head so he could look into her eyes with an intensity that twisted her heart into a tight ball. 'You wanted honesty, Clare, and that's what I've given you. I want that for us. I don't want secrets. I don't want anything we can't work our way through—*together*. Because if we can't do that—'

With a calmness that belied the pain she felt, Clare peeled his hands from her face. 'This is a lot, Quinn. I can't—'

'Yes, you can.' The words were said on a harsh whisper. 'You just have to want to.'

It wasn't that she didn't want to. She wanted to with all her heart and soul. From the very second they'd started down the path they'd taken she'd known she didn't want to lose him. She still didn't. But she needed time to think, to piece everything together, to work her way through it all…

To find a way to get past her shattered illusions of the relationship they'd had—and the relationships she had with all the people she'd come to love as friends. He'd just shaken her little world to pieces.

She lifted her chin. 'Do you trust me?'

Quinn looked suspicious. 'You know I do.'

'Do you trust me to make the right decision for me?'

'Why?'

'Because if you do, you need to trust me enough to give me some time with this; it's a *lot*. You know it is. And you can't land it in my lap and not give me time to think it through.'

'Right, I get it.' Then he quirked a dark brow. 'So what's the time limit this time?'

Clare gasped. 'Don't you dare. You *lied* to me.'

'There's still no grey area with you, is there? I could have gone a lifetime without telling you this.'

'What I didn't know wouldn't hurt me?'

*'Yes!'* He threw the word at her in frustration. 'Because you'd already been hurt enough! You think I ever wanted to cause you the kind of pain he did? *Why* would I want to do that?'

'It wasn't pain.' Clare shook her head. 'It was *humiliation.* I got it so completely wrong, don't you see? I didn't know him well enough to follow him all the way over here, let alone marry him!'

'Then why did you?'

*'I wish I knew!'* Just like that the tears came. Clare moaned in frustration. 'Damn it, Quinn, that's exactly why I need to think this time. Don't you get it? I'm not some starry-eyed dreamer any more. If I was, let me tell you, this would have knocked it out of me. It's not just that you lied—you *all* lied. I've never felt like such—like such an *outsider* before. I need to deal with that. So, please, let me do it.'

'I'm just supposed to wait for you to make the decision for both of us, am I? If you say it's over then it's over?'

'Like you do in every relationship you've ever been in?' She'd said it in the heat of the moment. It was uncalled for and she knew it, but it was too late to take it back. Quinn shut himself off before her very eyes, the control she'd always respected in him sliding into place like a shield.

Only this time she didn't respect it—she hated it.

'This'll be a dose of that thing called karma, won't it?' He even smiled a small smile. 'Well, while you're going through that decision-making process of yours maybe you'll think about why it is I've laid all this on the line for you tonight. And why it is I'm trying harder to make this relationship work than I ever did any of the others.'

Clare folded her arms across her thundering heart as he carried on. 'There was never going to be a right time to tell you all this, and believe me I searched for a right time. But I can't change the past, Clare, even if I wanted to. I can't tell you I wouldn't do it all over again either. Because I would—every damn time.'

When she gaped at him he jerked his shoulders. 'I am what I am. You wanted to know me better—well, now you know it all: the good *and* the bad. If I'm not what you want then I can't change that.'

She watched with wide eyes as he smiled meaningfully. 'I'd have a damn good try at it, though, don't get me wrong. If I'd been the kind of slime you thought I was, however briefly, along the way then I'd have been doing everything I could to tie you to me emotionally and physically these few weeks. But I haven't made love to you, no matter how much I wanted to, because I didn't want anything between us when it happened. More fool me, huh?'

He turned near the steps to the elevators, taking a deep breath before continuing. 'I'll take you home. Or wherever it is you plan on going.'

After a long moment of silent defiance she unfolded her arms and walked over to him, carrying her chin higher, but watching him from the corner of her eye. She was in front of him when he added, 'And to think I did all this tonight to reassure you the six week cut-off doesn't exist for us. I got that one wrong, didn't I? Only difference this time is it isn't me ending it. Guess I won the bet.'

Clare stopped and turned her face to look up at him;

Quinn's gaze was fixed on a point above her head. She watched him blink lazily a few times, searched what she could see of the vivid blue of his eyes but saw nothing. She hated the fact that he could hold himself together the way he was. But then she looked down and saw the pulse jump in the taut cord of his neck and she saw a tremor in his breathing. It was then she knew he was hurting as much as she was. It was the worst argument they'd ever had.

When she lifted her lashes she found him looking down at her, and when he looked back to the point over her head she took a deep breath and told him in a low, soft voice, 'I won't hate you. No matter how hard you try to make me.'

She heard him exhale, as if she'd just knocked the wind out of him. Then his chin dropped while he took several breaths before raising his lashes. 'The driver will take you wherever you want to go.'

'I'm going to Madison's for tonight, to give us both time to cool down.'

'Right.'

'Because this is the worst fight we've ever had.'

'Yeah.'

'And right now we're just making it worse.'

'Uh-huh.'

She frowned at him. 'You're being like this because you're hurting from it just as much as I am.'

Quinn blew air out through puffed cheeks before lifting his chin and looking her straight in the eye. 'Are we done here?'

It was a loaded question. One she didn't have an answer for.

# CHAPTER THIRTEEN

'YOU'VE REALLY MADE a mess this time, haven't you?'

Shouldering his way into Madison's apartment, Quinn ignored the other occupants in the room. 'Where is she?'

Morgan stood up. 'What do you want her for?'

Quinn frowned hard at him. 'Butt out, Morgan—*where is she*?'

'Not this time.' Morgan squared off against him, folding his arms and spreading his feet. 'Just how exactly are you planning on making this right? Do you have any idea how upset she was?'

'If she's here you know I'm moving you out of the way to get to her, right?'

Morgan jutted his chin. 'You could *try*.'

When Quinn sidestepped, Evan and Erin appeared, each of them assuming the same crossed-arms pose that said they meant business. Quinn practically growled at them, lifting both arms and dropping them to his sides before he asked in a raised voice, 'How am I supposed to fix this if you won't let me talk to her?'

'It took you all night to come up with a plan, did it?'

He glared at Evan. 'She needed time to *think*!'

Erin blinked at him. 'And her time's up now, is it? You're over here to bully her into forgiving you?'

Quinn scrubbed a large hand over his face and began to pace the room, grumbling under his breath. 'I don't need this.'

Madison's voice sounded from the door. 'It took from the early hours of this morning to talk everything through with her, you know.'

His head jerked up. *'Everything?'*

'Oh, she wouldn't discuss how she feels about *you*—seems you've infected her with that privacy disease of yours.' She shrugged. 'It took all that time for her to understand why none of the rest of us ever told her about you and Jamie. Worst eight hours of my life. She feels like we saw her as some kind of outsider. When the truth is we couldn't love her any more if we tried.'

There was a chorus of agreement from around the room, and then Morgan added, 'We all messed up. But she understands.'

'She does?'

'Jamie humiliated her on a grand scale—we should never have let it come to that. You were the only one who did anything about it.' Evan paused. 'We told her about the arguments we all had—how none of us could look her in the eye. And we told her you wanted her told from the get go.'

Quinn's eyes widened.

Erin confirmed Evan's words. 'We did. Though *you* could have told her that and it might have helped. But that's you all over, isn't it? We were the ones who told you to leave it alone—that it was none of our business. That made us guiltier of a lie of omission than you were. At least you *did something.*'

*'I had to.'* The confession was torn from so deep inside it came out in a croak.

'We told her that.' Madison's voice softened. 'She said she understood why. Don't suppose you want to tell *us* why, do you?'

Quinn shook his head. *Not so much.*

Morgan's large hand landed on his shoulder and squeezed in response. 'I think I know why.'

Erin ducked her head to look up into his eyes. 'Would it be okay if Morgan told us why?'

Quinn shrugged, despite the fact he'd just been spoken to as if he were a nine-year-old. 'If it's important you know.'

'It is. We do love you, you know. No matter how much of an idiot you can be.'

It honestly felt as if everyone on the planet was trying to rip his heart out with their bare hands. But Quinn nodded, the ache in his chest making it difficult for him to breathe, never mind find words. He just couldn't breathe properly until…

He lifted a fist to his chest and rubbed at it with his knuckles. And shifted his gaze in time to see Madison watching the tell-tale action. Her mouth twitched. 'Heart aching a tad there, big guy?'

He smiled ruefully. 'Where is she?'

'Went looking for you, funnily enough…'

Quinn's smile grew.

Erin laughed at his expression. 'You still here?'

Madison waited until he'd left before holding a palm out, waggling her fingers as a satisfied smile formed on her lips. 'Ante up, boys.'

Hands disappeared into pockets, and Morgan grumbled as he slapped a note into her hand. 'Never should've gone double or nothing on it being Clare he ended up with…'

Clare was sitting on his stoop when Quinn ran down the street, her knees drawn up high and her arms hugging them while she rested her chin. When she saw him she swallowed hard, her eyes following him until he stood in front of her. Chest heaving, he looked at her with an almost pained expression. Clare couldn't seem to find the right words, no matter how many times she'd thought about what she'd say when she saw him.

In the end he broke the tension. 'Hello, you.'

Clare took a sharp, shuddering breath, her vision blurring at the edges. 'Hello, you.'

'You scared me.'

The confession surprised her. 'Did I?'

'Uh-huh.' He nodded.

'You scared me by not being here. I thought you skipped town on me again.' Her brows wavered in question. 'Where were you?'

'Looking for you.' She watched his throat convulse. 'I needed to tell you something. But we need to talk about all this other stuff first. Lay it to rest.'

With some considerable effort she found a voice barely recognizable as hers. 'We do.'

Quinn took a step closer and hunched down in front of her. He nodded, he frowned, and then he studied her hair.

Clare couldn't help but smile affectionately at him, her voice threaded with emotion. 'It'll involve the use of words.'

Quinn grimaced. 'Yeah, well, I'm still not so hot on

those when it comes to the things that matter, so you might have to give me a minute. I already messed up royally last night; I don't want to do that to us again.'

'Would it help if I started?'

'Might.' He smiled a somewhat crooked smile.

'Okay…' she took a deep breath '…you should have told me you wanted to tell me about Jamie but the others convinced you not to. It might have helped.'

'They mentioned that when I went looking for you.'

'You went to Madison's?'

'I did.'

'Did they tell you we spent hours talking?'

'They did.' When his eyes shadowed she smiled a somewhat watery smile at him. 'They said it helped.'

'It did.' Her lower lip shook, so she bit down on it. 'I just needed to work it through with a neutral party. I'm sorry.'

'It's okay.'

She was never going to make it all the way through everything she needed to say if he kept looking at her the way he was. In all the time she'd known him she'd never once seen such intense warmth in his eyes. It made her want to crawl into him, wrap herself around him, and stay there until she didn't hurt any more.

'There were too many grey areas for there to be a right or a wrong. It was unfair that you were all put in that position in the first place. I know why you did what you did, Quinn.' She swallowed down the lump in her throat before continuing in a broken voice. 'You did it because you couldn't stand by and watch another woman treated the way your mother was. It was too close to home for you. Being so close to Jamie, you thought you could make him see sense. You thought you could fix it, didn't you?'

Thick lashes flickered as he searched her eyes, and then he nodded, almost as if he was afraid to say yes in case he got it wrong.

'When you couldn't fix everything, you gave up one of your closest friends and tried to make up for his mistakes by looking after me.'

'It might have started out that way, yes.'

The first fat tears tripped over her lower lashes and blazed a heated trail down her cheeks. 'It's what you do. It's not like I was your first damsel in distress…'

'You're the only one that mattered *to me.*'

'Once you'd had time to get to know me.'

'There was no strategy, I swear.' His mouth quirked. 'I wasn't anywhere near that clever.'

More silent tears slid free, and Clare saw the flash of pain in his eyes as he followed their path. 'You didn't like me much at the beginning, did you?'

He sighed heavily. 'I wasn't supposed to notice you at all. When someone's engaged to someone she's automatically off limits. I just didn't understand what you were doing with him, was all.'

Not that it would have made a difference even if he *had* noticed her; he would never have broken the code of honour that ran so deeply in him. Clare loved him for that—he would never, ever cheat on her, or so much as look at another woman sideways. When he made a commitment it would be for life, wouldn't it?

'I didn't love him, Quinn. It was…I guess it was just the adventure of it: whole new life, new country. I was very starry-eyed back then. But when I got here I was more in love with the city than I was with him. I think I knew I didn't feel enough when I was able to stand in front of all those people that day. It wasn't heartbreak I felt—it was just complete and utter humiliation.' She paused to take another shaky breath. 'But I don't think anyone really knows they're in love until it's the real thing. Then it's the only thing that really matters. I know that now. And I'm not sorry I came here…'

When he frowned she tried to find the words to make him understand. 'If I hadn't, I would never have met you. It's because of you I know the difference…'

Clare damped her lips, took another shuddering breath and felt another tear slide free. And while Quinn looked at her with intense, consuming heat in his vivid eyes, she let the words slip free on a husky whisper. 'I love you.'

It was as if a dam burst. Hiccupping sobs sounded and tears streamed while she said it more firmly. 'You really have no idea how much I love you.'

For a moment Quinn froze, and then his gruff voice demanded, 'Say it again.'

'I love you.' Somehow she managed to smile. It was weak and tremulous, but it was the best she could do. 'I can't breathe properly when you're not there.'

Large hands framed her face and he kissed her as a man would drink water after a long spell in the desert. The vibration of the groan that rumbled up from his chest awakened every nerve-ending she possessed until she ached from head to toe with the need to get closer. So she did what she'd wanted to do. She crawled into him, wrapping her arms around his neck and pushing her breasts tight to the wall of his chest as they slowly came to their feet. But it still wasn't close enough for

Clare—even when his hands dropped and he squeezed her waist tight enough to break her in half.

Her mouth followed his when he lifted his head and looked down at her with an incredulity that made her smile. 'Say it again.'

Clare's smile grew, her heart swelling to impossible proportions in her chest. 'I love you.'

The smile he gave her made her laugh. But instead of kissing her again he let go of her and tangled his fingers with hers, tugging her up the steps. 'Come on.'

Less than a minute later she was being steered across the hardwood floors into his study, where he pushed her into the leather chair behind his desk and hunched in front of her again.

'I've got something for you.'

Clare was vaguely aware of him pulling open the top drawer and reaching for something. But she was too mesmerized by him to look away. Too enthralled by how happy he looked. Too much in love to want to look anywhere else…

'Here.' Something was set into her hands.

When he looked expectantly at her she smiled and looked down, her gaze rising sharply when she saw what it was. 'You're giving me my goodbye gift *now*?'

'Open it.' He reached out and brushed tendrils of hair off her cheeks with his fingertips. Clare loved it when he did that.

She tugged at the white ribbon while still staring at him, only dropping her chin when she had the lid off. Inside was a smaller box covered in dark velvet.

Quinn smiled a smile that made the blue of his eyes darken to the colour of stormy tropical seas.

'Keep going.'

There was a slight creak as she opened the second box. Her gaze dropped as its content was revealed to her amazed eyes. Heart pounding erratically, she jerked her chin up, gaze tangling impossibly with his. And what she could see there stopped her heart, tore it loose from her chest…and allowed it to soar…

'My last Tiffany's box.'

Clare smiled dumbly.

The voice she loved so very much was impossibly tender when he told her; 'I love you back.'

Her smile trembled again. 'You never use that word.'

'I don't think you should unless you mean it.'

'I know you think that.' She lifted a hand and rested her palm against his face. When Quinn exhaled and closed his eyes as he leaned into her touch she saw her vision mist all over again.

His eyes flickered open. 'You crept up on me, and I like to think I fought a good fight, but I love you. I know they say that living together and working together is the kiss of death for a relationship, but I want to spend every minute of every day with you. And since I'm not good with words, I want to spend pretty much all night every night keeping you awake so I can *show you* how I feel—*lots.*'

A threatening sob magically morphed into a hiccup of laughter and she let her fingertips smooth against a hint of stubble on his cheek, turning her hand to draw the backs of her fingers along his jawline.

'And when I tire you out enough for you to sleep I want to wake up in the morning with you beside me. I want to be told off for not using a coaster and I want daisies everywhere, and I—'

She smiled at him. 'You had me at *I love you back.* Ask me the question.'

Quinn apparently felt the need to kiss her into a boneless heap before he did, just to be sure. So it was amidst a state of sensory bliss that she heard not a question, but another demand. 'Marry me.'

She loved him. She would love him till the day she died. He loved her. There was only the one answer. 'Yes.' The box still held firmly between her fingers, she wrapped the crook of her arm around his neck. 'And not just because I love you. But because I need you as much as you need me. It's your turn to be rescued this time. I'm rescuing you.'

'I'm okay with that.' He pressed a light kiss on her lips while reaching for the box to extricate the ring. 'And you're right, I do need you. You're so tangled up in my life now that I can't breathe right when you're not around either.'

The fact it was said with a husky crackling in his already gruff voice told Clare a million things about the depth of his feelings that words could never have conveyed. He needed her every bit as much as she needed him—they were a perfect match.

Using her right hand to tilt his chin up while he reached for her left, Clare informed him, 'It's a Lucida, by the way. The Tiffany setting you have that enormous diamond in.'

'You said diamonds were a girl's best friend. That's apart from me, obviously…'

'Obviously.'

Amusement danced in his eyes. 'You have all the Tiffany settings memorized, don't you?'

Clare bobbed her head. 'Pretty much. Everyone has a hobby.'

'I'm in love with a crazy girl.'

'And she's crazy in love with you.'

And there was no niggling doubt in Clare's mind, no fear for the future, and, yes, her starry eyes were back. But Quinn had put the stars there. He was her soulmate in oh, so many ways. The thought made her grin as he slipped the ring onto her finger.

'You know what this means, don't you?'

She leaned forward, placing her hands on his chest to push him backwards as she slid off the chair and onto him; stretching her body along the length of his.

'What does it mean?' Quinn smiled as he pushed long fingers into her hair and drew her face towards his, where Clare whispered the answer against his lips.

'I win.'

# EPILOGUE

'HELLO, YOU.'

Clare grinned at Quinn's reflection as he walked up behind her, one long arm snaking around her waist while his head lowered to the hollow where her neck met her shoulder. 'Hello, me.'

Quinn spread his feet and pulled her against his lean body, pressing a row of kisses along the neck she angled for him. 'You ready?'

'Mmm-hmm.' She lifted her hands and set them on his arm, leaning her head back against his shoulder. 'You?'

He'd kissed his way to the sensitive skin below her ear before he lifted inky lashes and his gaze met hers, his rough voice vibrating against her ear. 'I love you.'

Clare smiled softly. 'Getting easier to say that word, isn't it?'

'Practice makes perfect.'

Turning in his arms, she stood on her toes and kissed him. 'Love you back.'

'Course you do.' He bent his knees and lifted her off the ground, turning on his heel to head back towards the door. 'I'm irresistible.'

'At the risk of making it difficult for you to get your head through doors I'm going to have to agree with that.' She wrapped her arms around his neck and looked down at him. 'So, are you telling them or am I?'

'I am. You can fend off all the hugs and kisses.'

'You're still a work in progress, you know.'

'You can work on me more later…' He set her down by the door and studied her incredible emerald eyes for the longest time. 'Do you need a minute?'

'No.' She kissed him again.

It never ceased to amaze Quinn, as he looked at her, how he could love her more with each passing day. He hadn't known it could be like that. But then he hadn't known anything about love until Clare.

It felt as if nobody had ever known him till she knew him, touched him till she touched him—loved him till she loved him. She was air to him now. Without her he wouldn't exist. Turned out he was a romantic after all.

'Okay. Here goes.'

With her fine-boned fingers tangled in his, they walked to the front of the room. Quinn eventually gave up on the waved-arm method in favour of placing his thumb and forefinger between his teeth and whistling. It got everyone's attention a lot faster.

When he looked down at Clare she was laughing at what he'd done, so he winked at her before lifting his chin and clearing his throat.

'Thanks for coming—especially those of you who travelled so far. We appreciate it.' His smile grew. 'But I'm afraid you're not here for an engagement party. You're here for a wedding…'

Return to Virgin River with a breathtaking new trilogy from award-winning author

# ROBYN CARR

February 2009

March 2009

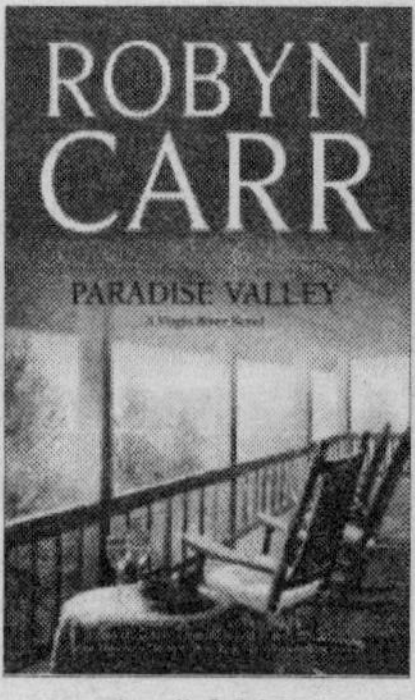


April 2009

"The Virgin River books are so compelling—
I connected instantly with the characters
and just wanted more and more and more."
—#1 *New York Times* bestselling author
Debbie Macomber

MIRA®

**www.MIRABooks.com**

MRCTRI09